"You okay?" he said, his breath in her hair as she slightly staggered, then righted herself, The Bump knocking against him.

"Of course," she said, meeting his gaze. And this time, his eyes weren't twinkling. This time, she saw...more. Confusion, maybe. Lust, definitely, which almost made her laugh out loud, considering she felt about as sexy as a bag of potatoes.

Mostly, though, she saw yearning. For what, she wasn't sure. And neither was he, she imagined. But that longing...it not only touched her heart, but came awfully close to breaking it—

"Hey, lovebirds!" said some paunchy dude on the sidewalk. "If it's okay with you, I'd like to get to my car sometime today?"

"Sure, no problem," Tyler said, setting Laurel aside to slam shut the open door, then hustling her toward the restaurant before Irked Dude ruptured something. She wasn't sure whether to be relieved or hugely annoyed.

Once inside, however, where they had to wait in the jammed lobby for a free table, she got over herself enough to realize hunger—and, okay, a still-bruised heart—had momentarily made her hallucinate, seeing and hearing things that weren't there. The longing, yes—that, she hadn't imagined. But not a longing for *her.* Big difference.

But you know what? Tyler had already proven himself a good friend. Someone she could rely on. Could trust. And right now, a *friend* is what she needed, more than anything.

And if she kept telling herself that, she might almost believe it.

Dear Reader,

I'm sure nearly every woman reading this has thought at some point—after asking a spouse/spawn/underling for the thousandth time for help with something—"You know what? Forget it. I'll just do it myself." Because so often that seems like the easier, and less stressful, route to take, right? Except then we not only burden ourselves with all the stuff we shouldn't be doing, but we're denying others the opportunity to step up to the plate.

Not an easy lesson to learn, though. Especially for Laurel Kent, who, after being left in the lurch far too often by people she should have been able to count on, has decided going it alone is much more preferable to putting her trust in somebody else... and then being disappointed. What she doesn't realize, however, is that by letting Tyler Noble into her and her baby boy's life, she's actually giving her cutie-patootie younger neighbor the chance to grow from man-child to man...and to be far more than either one of them would have ever expected him to be. And that's never a bad thing. ;-)

I hope you enjoy this story of unexpected opportunity and answered dreams as much as I loved telling it.

Blessings,

Karen Templeton

More Than
She Expected

—

Karen Templeton

HARLEQUIN® SPECIAL EDITION®

Recycling programs
for this product may
not exist in your area.

ISBN-13: 978-0-373-65806-0

MORE THAN SHE EXPECTED

Copyright © 2014 by Karen Templeton-Berger

Printed in U.S.A.

KAREN TEMPLETON

A recent inductee into the Romance Writers of America Hall of Fame, three-time RITA® Award-winning author Karen Templeton has written more than thirty novels for Harlequin. She lives in New Mexico with two hideously spoiled cats, has raised five sons and lived to tell the tale, and could not live without dark chocolate, mascara and Netflix.

To Kotie-Pie, my niece's squishably adorable boxer
Who provided the inspiration for Boomer.

And to my many Facebook friends
Who are always ready
To answer any and all of my dumb questions.
You guys are a lot more fun than Google.

Chapter One

Lightning stabbed Tyler's eyes an instant before thunder slammed through the house, rattling windows and propelling him off the sofa and through his kitchen to wrench open the patio door. When he'd let the dog out ten minutes ago, it'd been calm and sunny, a perfect June day—

"Boomer! Come on in, buddy!"

But all he heard was the wind ripping at the trees, another skull-shattering thunderclap. Swearing, Tyler stomped out onto the worn deck overlooking his paltry backyard, the sky so black he half expected to see flying monkeys—

"Boomer!" he yelled again, blinking against the brutal wind. This was nuts—how the hell did you lose an eighty-pound dog? Especially one who normally waited out thunderstorms wedged under the bed. Or, more often, against Tyler. "Dammit, mutt—where *are* you?"

He tromped off the deck and around to the side yard,

dodging airborne leaves. From behind a wall of tangled, overgrown pyracantha and Virginia creeper the rickety wooden fence shuddered and groaned, bitching at him for not having fixed it yet. A windsurfing plastic bag plastered to his chest; Tyler snatched it off, balling it up and stuffing it into his pocket as thunder cracked again, too close, making him jump. Where the *hell* was the dog?

Not in the well leading out from the basement. Or behind the small shed. Or under the deck...

His heart pounding so hard it hurt, Tyler called again as a bodacious raindrop pinged his forehead, instantly followed by a billion of its cousins. Swearing, Ty shoved through the jungle and out the side gate to the front yard, even though it wasn't like the dog could open the latch, for God's sake—

"BOOMER!" Ty bellowed, hands cupped around his mouth, water streaming down his face, into his eyes—

"Over here!"

Tyler jerked left, then right—

"Behind you! On the porch!"

He whipped around. And there was his damn dog, shivering to beat the band in his neighbor's arms—Laurel, he thought she'd said her name was when she'd moved in a few months ago. Floppy ears slicked back, stubby tail quivering, Boomer ducked his smooth, solid head when he saw Tyler, his amber eyes shining like a pair of lights in his sweet, black face.

Soaked, but hugely relieved, Tyler unhooked the short iron gate and forded the instant river surging across the bumpy cement walk. The house was a mirror image of his, a sturdy little Craftsman one-story with a dormered attic, a decent porch. Pretty typical small-town Jersey. Except Laurel's was all dollhouse colors, pale yellow and blue, where Ty's was dark and manly. Or something.

"He was scratching at my door," Laurel said over the rain thrumming on her porch overhang as she smiled at the idiot dog. Dumbass was eating it up, too, licking her face while his butt wiggled so hard it blurred. Laughing, Laurel leaned back on her heels, only to let out an "Oh!" when Boomer knocked her flat on her can.

"Crap, I'm so sorry!" Ty grabbed the dog's collar, tugging him off the poor woman before she drowned in dog spit. "Get over here—"

"It's okay," Laurel said, getting to her feet, still grinning even as she scrubbed the collar of her baggy overshirt across her jaw. Her standard getup, usually worn with those stretchy pants or tights or whatever they were, from what little Ty'd seen of her. He only had a few inches on her, he realized, her nothing-else-but brown hair not short, but not long, either. And straight as a stick, like his was, even in the humidity. She was okay-looking, he supposed, but not what you'd call a knockout.

Except then she met his gaze dead-on, and he nearly tripped over his own dog. While standing completely still. To say her eyes were blue was like… Okay, if angels had blue eyes? They'd be this color—

"Boomer—is that right?—is a real sweetheart. What is he?"

Tyler snapped back to attention. "Mostly boxer. With a little Rottie in there for bulk. And he's my *boy,* aren't you, you big stinker?" he said, taking the dog's head in his hands to kiss the top of his head. The dog woofed, jowls flapping around his ridiculous underbite, and Tyler caught Laurel's look of tolerant amusement. A lot like the one his adoptive mother used to give him when he'd screw up. Which'd been about every five minutes there at the beginning.

"What? I love my dog."

Laurel laughed again—a nice sound, low in her chest.

"I can see that. And this is embarrassing. I know you told me your name when we met—"

"Sorry. Tyler," he said, slicking back his wet hair. "Tyler Noble. And you're Laurel, right? Laurel… Hold on…" Grinning, he pointed at her. "Kent."

"Yeah. Wow. Good memory."

For women's names? You bet. A skill Ty'd been fine-honing since those first hormones blinked their sleepy eyes when he was ten or eleven or something and whispered, *You're all ours, now.* Also, he'd been far more curious about his reclusive neighbor than he should probably admit. She rarely left the house, far as he knew. Not that he was around much during the week, usually, but since his salvage shop wasn't far he often came home for lunch, and her old Volvo wagon was always in the driveway. And the only visitor he'd seen was some old lady who drove a spiffy new Prius—

Boomer slurped his tongue across Ty's hand, earning him a glare. "He hates thunderstorms, so why—let alone how—he got out, I have no idea."

"Um…this isn't the first time he's paid a visit."

Tyler's eyes shot to hers. "You're kidding?"

"Nope." Now, despite the smile—no lipstick, fullish mouth—Ty noticed the caution shimmering in those eyes. And the crows' feet fanning out from them. A couple years older than him, maybe. So…mid-thirties or thereabouts—?

"So you don't let him roam the neighborhood?"

"What? No!" He looked at Boomer, who'd planted his posterior on the porch floor and was noisily yawning, then back at Laurel, who was somehow getting prettier every time he looked at her. Except she wasn't his type. He was almost sure. Nor was he hers, he was even more sure—

"The fence!" Ty said, snapping his fingers. "I'll bet there's a hole under it somewhere."

"Oh. Maybe so. And I don't have a gate on my side yard. Although why he doesn't just knock on my *back* door, I have no idea."

She smiled again, and Ty's brain checked out for a moment. "Uh…yeah. Yeah." *Dude! Really?* "Soon as it stops raining, I'll check it. Get that sucker fixed so my dog stops bothering you."

Laurel's gaze dipped to the dog. "Oh. Well, yes, I suppose you should fix the fence, but…" Her eyes bounced back up to his. Still blue. Still incredible. "Actually, I don't mind the company." A long pause preceded, "Um…would you like to come in? I could make tea or something…?"

Way in the distance, thunder softly rumbled. The storm was moving off.

As should you, buddy.

"Nah, thanks, but I'm soaked to the skin. And in case you didn't notice, my dog stinks. Anyway, you're probably busy.…"

A smile flitted across her lips as she tugged that floppy shirt closed. It'd been a weirdly cool June anyway; now, in the wake of the storm, the damp breeze was downright frigid. "No problem. Another time, then."

"Uh…sure." Because that's what you said when both parties knew "another time" was never going to happen. Especially once he found, and plugged up, somebody's little escape hatch. He grabbed the dog's collar and began tugging him down the porch steps, tossing, "You have a good night, okay?" over his shoulder as he made what felt weirdly like an escape.

Laurel watched as Tyler and the dog trudged back to his house, then let out a whew-that-was-close sigh that fogged around her face in the chilly, damp air. Because, really, what had she been thinking, inviting the man in for tea? If he even drank tea, which she seriously doubted.

Hormones, that's all this was. Had to be. Only reason she could see for her insane, and totally inappropriate, attraction to her cute, sexy, built, sexy, blond, sexy neighbor.

Her cute, sexy, built, blond *obviously younger* neighbor, who clearly had a thing for cute, sexy, blonde, *petite,* obviously-younger-than-he-was girls. Not that they were talking dozens or anything. And Laurel supposed they'd all—well, all *two,* and not at the same time, to be fair—had seemed nice enough from what she could tell through her living room window. If a little overzealous in the giggling department. One of them, anyway. Who giggled enough for five girls, honestly. But the thing was, they were obviously nothing like Laurel. Nor she, them. Being neither blonde nor petite. Not to mention sexy. So she somehow doubted Tyler would ever be interested in her, in any case.

Even if she weren't, you know. Knocked up.

Shaking her head at herself, Laurel yanked open her storm door and went back inside, where the symphony of Easter egg colors on her walls, her furnishings, made her smile. Yes, the house was a work in progress, but it was *her* work in progress. So, bam. Three months since she'd signed the mortgage papers, and she still couldn't quite believe it, that she'd thrown caution to the winds and bought a *house.*

Her hand went to her belly, still barely pooched out underneath her roomy top. Speaking of throwing caution to the winds.

But as she walked through the still, silent space, the realization that it wouldn't be still and silent for very long made her smile. Especially when she came to what would be the baby's room. Where, leaning against the doorjamb, she shuddered, from a combination of giddy anticipation and sheer terror. As well as the ugliest shade of mauve known to man. *Thank you, 1983,* she thought, then sighed. Definitely not how she'd envisioned becoming a mother. Sure, Gran would want to help, but Marian McKinney was well into her eighties, for heaven's sake. Mentally spry, for sure, but Laurel doubted the old girl was up to chasing a toddler—a thought that sent another shiver down Laurel's spine.

To say this was unexpected didn't even begin to cover it. But here she was, pregnant, and alone, and you know what? She could either moan and groan about cruel fate or whatever, or she could suck it up, count her blessings— which were many, actually—and make the best damn lemonade, ever.

She smiled. Maybe she should paint the room yellow, like lemonade. Or sunshine—

Her doorbell rang. Frowning, Laurel tromped back down the hall and peered through the peephole, her heart bumping when she saw Tyler. Honestly.

"Found the problem," he said when she opened the door, all business with his arms crossed high on his chest. He wore his hair long enough that a breeze had shoved a hunk of streaked blond hair across his forehead, making him look about sixteen. The kind of sixteen-year-old boy that made mamas of sixteen-year-old girls chew their nails to the quick. "Wanna come see?"

"Um, sure—"

"You might want to put on some heavier shoes, though," he said, nodding at her flimsy ballet flats. "It's pretty wet out there."

Her feet duly shoved into already-tied sneakers, she followed her neighbor around to her backyard, which desperately needed mowing. Yeah, she'd get right on that. Tyler pointed to a spot near the back corner where the wooden fence leaned especially badly. A lot worse than when she'd moved in, which was saying something. But, hey, it helped her negotiate a lower price, so there ya go.

"Ah." Laurel sighed. "Guess this means I need to finally fix my fence."

"Since he's going *under* the fence, that wouldn't help."

She frowned at her neighbor. Who actually glowed in the sunlight. Dear God. "You never noticed the hole on your side?"

"Um…" He clasped the back of his neck. "I might have a slight…bush problem there. Anyway…here's my idea. Even if I trim back the jungle, and you fix your fence, and we fill the hole back up, dog's probably just gonna dig a new hole, right? So what I'm thinking is, how's about I build a cinder block wall instead?"

Laurel made a face. "Prison chic? I'm thinking no."

Tyler laughed. And, natch, he had a great laugh. And dimples. Right out of the devil's toolbox, those dimples. "Doesn't have to be gray, there's all kinds of colors now. Since I've got brick, anyway, on the other two sides, maybe something that'll kinda match? Then you can ditch that thing—" he nodded at the pathetic wood fence "—and not have to worry about another one for a long, long time. If ever."

Man had a point. "I suppose that might work. When could you do it?"

"Next weekend, if it doesn't rain?" Then he grinned at her. And winked. "You can help, if you want."

Oh, hell…he was *flirting?* Then again, flirting was probably his default mode. Part of his genetic makeup, like the surfer blond hair. And—she couldn't help but notice—the gold-flecked hazel eyes, twinkling in the late-afternoon sunlight…

Sighing—at her own foolishness, mostly—Laurel forced her gaze away from those twinkling eyes and back to the muddy hole. A symbol of her life if ever there was one. "Not sure I'd be much good," she muttered. Which would have been true even if she hadn't been pregnant. Upper body strength was not her strong suit. Then, mustering her courage, she looked at him again. "You can really build a wall?"

Ty put his hand on his heart, looking stricken. "Aww... you don't trust me?"

"Since we're talking many hundreds of pounds that could potentially topple over on my..." She caught herself. "On me, it seems prudent to ask."

"Fair enough. But yeah, I can. A damn good one, too. Got my start working construction, first year was doing masonry—"

"Is there something you could show me? So I could see your work for myself?"

"Wow. Tough customer. Nobody's gonna pull one over on you, huh?"

He should only know. "Just being practical. Well?"

He shoved his hands into his jeans pockets. "Actually...I built one for...someone not that long ago. She doesn't live too far away. I could take you over to see it, if you like. You could even push on it, make sure it stays put." When she laughed, he added, "Afterwards, how's about we go pick out the blocks together? So you get the color you want. Because I don't care, frankly."

"Sounds like a plan. But...since it's a shared wall, and you're going to be doing all the work, at least let me pay for the blocks."

"And since we wouldn't be doing this if it weren't for my dog, I'm gonna have to say 'no' to that."

"Don't be silly. If I can't physically help, the least I can do is contribute to the cost. Which I would've done, anyway. No, I mean it," she said to his snort. "I won't feel right otherwise."

That got a long, assessing look before he finally said, "How about a home-cooked meal in exchange? Would that work?"

A laugh pushed through her nose. "Considering my extreme lack of culinary skills? Probably not."

Ty looked so disappointed she nearly laughed again. "You don't cook?"

"As in, taking random ingredients and turning them into something palatable? Not so much." She paused, then said, "But since I do eat—" Every hour, on the hour, these days. Not something he needed to know. Or that the idea of Tyler Noble sitting at her kitchen table made her slightly dizzy. "—I'm sure I can come up with something. That's why God made delis, right?"

He grinned. An endearing grin, the kind that probably turned his mother to goo when he was a kid. Since it was making Laurel more than a little gooey herself. "Absolutely."

She smiled back, then took a deep breath—because she had a hunch whatever was going on here had precious little to do with being neighborly, and what on earth was she supposed to do with that?—and said, "So…when can we go see this wall?"

His smile dimmed slightly. But only for a moment. "I'll give her a call, see if we can go over sometime tomorrow. If that works for you?"

"Absolutely," Laurel said.

Because the sooner they got this little folderol over with, the better.

His butt-ugly face wedged between the bucket seats, Boomer alternated hot-breath panting with slurping in his drool as Tyler pulled his pickup into Starla's short drive-way. On the other side of the dog, Laurel sat with her giant purse on her lap, staring out the windshield. Ty didn't think she'd said ten words in the past ten minutes, despite her having been chatty enough the day before.

Normally this wouldn't be a problem—his teachers used to say he talked enough for ten people, anyway—but her silence was a touch unnerving. Was it him? Had he done or said something to make her clam up? Not that he should care. They were neighbors, that's all. Neighbors only going to look at a wall.

And besides, he could tell this one was classy. Not in a la-di-da, designer duds kind of way, but for real. Something Tyler had never been and never would be. Not that he was scum—although he'd skirted close enough, from time to time, to make his parents despair, he was sure—but no matter how often you prune a wildly growing bush in an attempt to tame it, its roots stay the same. Meaning, left to its own devices, it'll always revert to its wild nature. And while those wild roots didn't seem to be an issue for a lot of the women he'd known over the years, he was pretty sure they would be for Laurel.

So if his ego was whining because Laurel was apparently the first woman since his adoptive mother to be impervious to his blarney….well, his ego could shut the hell up, is what.

"Cute house," Laurel said, popping open the car door. Yesterday's storm had left behind clear blue skies and a cool, brisk breeze, making it feel more like fall than early summer. Starla's little white bungalow—a dream come true for her, he knew, thanks in no small part to a leg up from the state for first-time home buyers—gleamed in the strong afternoon sunshine, the new windows Tyler'd installed glimmering like diamonds.

"Yeah. It is," he said. Only he must've sounded funny, because Laurel gave him a weird look. But with a little shake of her head, she lowered herself from the passenger seat, the dog shoving past her and over to Starla, who'd come outside to greet them, all smiles as usual. She'd just gotten off work, still in jeans and a plain white polo shirt, her long blond hair pulled back from her still-pretty face. It was weird, how sometimes she looked far younger than her forty-eight years, while other times she seemed so much older.

The drugs' toll, he supposed.

Now she untangled herself from the dog's exuberant greeting to hold out her hand to Laurel. "So nice to meet you, honey! Can I get you something to drink? Iced tea? A Coke—?"

"We're only here to look at the wall," Tyler said quietly, reminding her.

Hazel eyes flashed to his. "What? She can't sip on a soda while she looks?"

Laurel smiled. "Thank you, but I'm fine. Really. Except...would you mind if I used your bathroom?"

"Not at all! Come on in..."

Tyler frowned. It'd barely been ten minutes, if that, since they'd left Laurel's house. And the plan—*his* plan—had been to show her the wall, let her shove on it, then get out again. Before anybody started asking questions. Questions he'd rather not answer, if he didn't have to.

His forehead still pinched, he followed the women—and his dog—inside, where Starla steered Laurel down the hall and Boomer moseyed on over to the sofa to mess with Mrs. Slocombe, Starla's megasized gray tabby. Who'd been peacefully napping until this dumb dog stuck his nose in her face—

"I take it she doesn't know?" Starla said behind him.

Tyler turned, leaving the hissing cat and barking dog to work it out between them. "Why should she? She's only my neighbor."

Starla crossed her arms over her rib cage, her gaze razor-sharp. A helluva lot more than it used to be, that was for sure. But there was a sadness behind the sharpness he couldn't deny. Especially because he'd put it there. At least partly.

"You've done so much for me, Ty," she said softly. "A lot more than I ever would have expected. So why can't you get past this? I mean, seriously—what difference does it make? It's not like it would change anything, right?"

As often as the subject came up, you'd think by now he'd be inured to the pain. The guilt that he couldn't let it go. And yes, the anger, since he'd *told* her why, every time she'd asked. And every time, they'd come to the same impasse, where she'd ask for forgiveness and he'd restate the conditions for her exoneration, and she'd give him the same, unsatisfactory answer—sometimes tearfully, sometimes wearily, often angrily—to the same nagging question:

"Who's my father?"

And he was hardly going to get into it again with Laurel right down the hall. In fact, he heard the door open, sensed her stop to glance at one of the few photos Starla had from before. Nothing that would mean anything to Laurel, he wouldn't imagine. Then she was there, in her skinny black pants and another floppy top in some blah color, no makeup, no jewelry, smiling at him—a friendly little grin, no biggee—and some crazy feeling that was almost unpleasant plowed right into his gut.

"All better?" Starla said.

"Much." Then, to Tyler: "So lead me to this wall."

"Sure," he said, taking her through Starla's orange-and-aqua kitchen, the window over the sink so choked with plants the light could barely get through, and out the sliding glass door. Like his, the yard wasn't much to speak of, the small, grassy plot balding in places. But Ty took a lot better care of Starla's yard than he did his own—since he didn't have time for both—and the blooming rosebushes crowded against the wall certainly seemed happy enough.

Wordlessly, Laurel tramped across the damp grass and, yes, pressed both palms against the wall. Then she sidled close between his mother's Mr. Lincoln and Chicago Peace and looked toward the far end—to check that it was straight, he assumed.

Then she gave him a thumb's-up, and he chuckled.

He heard the patio door slide open, saw Starla come out onto the tiny patio with a tray holding a pitcher, some glasses, a plate of something. She'd changed out of her work clothes into something flowy and long, her hair hanging loose. What she called her "hippy dippy" look. An homage of sorts to her long-dead parents, he supposed.

"I know, I know," she said, setting the tray on a small glass-topped table. "But if somebody doesn't help me eat these cookies, I'll end up sucking them all down myself. And that would be very bad."

"Cookies?" Laurel said, hustling across the yard.

"Butterscotch chocolate chip," Starla said, and Laurel looked like she might cry.

"You made these?"

"I sure did, honey."

Almost reverently, Laurel lifted one from the plate and took her first bite. "Oh. My. God. These are incredible!"

"Thank you!" Starla beamed. "It's my own recipe! Please—take as many as you want!"

Laurel laughed, that deep, genuine sound Ty was already coming to like way, way too much. "You might regret saying that," she said, and picked up two more. Without even a single, *"I really shouldn't…"*

"Here, let me put some in a bag for you…"

Starla scooted back inside, her dress billowing behind her, and Ty said, "You must be *really* hungry."

Laurel grinned…and chomped off another bite. "These are *really* good. I mean, insanely good. Here—" She held one out. "Taste it—"

"Not a huge fan of butterscotch, but thanks. You, however, have made Starla's day."

Her forehead crimped. "The cookies are wonderful. So I told her so. No big deal."

For her, maybe not.

Tyler thought about the girls he usually went with, with their done-up hair and made-up faces and pushed-up boobs, and how he'd always liked that, how they'd make all this effort to look good for him. How they'd have a little fun, for a little while, only then somebody would get bored, and it'd be all "No hard feelings, 'kay?" and that would be that. Because life was just easier with built-in expiration dates.

Except here comes this chick who clearly doesn't give a crap how she looks, she's not trying to impress anybody, especially not him, and suddenly it's all wham-a-bam-ding-dong inside his chest? What the hell?

Starla returned with a plastic zipper bag, filling it with most of the cookies as her instant fan kept on with the gushing. And Tyler had to admit, it wasn't exactly breaking him up, to see how happy that made the older woman. Who he knew hadn't had a whole lot of happy, for a very long time.

Not wanting to think about that, however, he returned his attention to Laurel. "So. Does my work meet your exacting standards?"

A breeze came up, sending a strand of hair into her mouth as she chewed. She yanked it out, making a face.

"Not that I know from walls, really, but…sure. Let's do this. You said the block yard's not far?"

"Maybe ten, fifteen minutes. Our houses are on the way, might as well drop off the dog. We can go ahead and order everything now, if you want."

"Sounds good." She hesitated. "Soon as I take another potty break." Another faint blush swept across her cheeks. "That's what I get for drinking way too much tea earlier, sorry."

He watched her walk back into the house, thinking, this was somebody who was cool with who she was. What she was. Who could talk about peeing without getting all coy about it…who Tyler guessed never faked anything. Which, even more than all the surface stuff, was why this wham-a-bam business was for the birds.

Because Tyler *didn't* know who he was. Not entirely. His whole life…it was like one big lie, wasn't it? Okay, maybe not a lie, exactly. A mystery, then.

He looked at Starla, snapping the top back on the cookie container, the only person in the world, as far as he knew, who held the key that would unlock that mystery. And until that happened—if it ever did—the Laurels of the world were strictly off-limits.

No matter how warm inside their laughs made him feel.

Chapter Two

"Mind if I put on some music?" Tyler asked when they got back in his truck. Because right now, his brain—among other things—needed to chill. And if he couldn't make Laurel stop smelling so good, or her eyes less blue, or her laugh less arousing, maybe music would distract him from noticing. At least, not as much.

"Not at all," she said, clutching her giant purse like it might make a break for it if she didn't. And yes, he caught the slight smile when, from his docked iPod, his favorite band started playing. Followed by an almost-imperceptible headshake.

"You don't like Green Day?" he asked.

"It's just been a while since I listened to them," she said, still with the irritating little smile. Tyler tapped the button on the steering wheel, turned the music off.

"No, it's okay, you don't have to—"

"Wasn't in the mood, anyway."

They reached the end of the block, turned onto the main drag. Behind them, the dog panted. Laurel shifted a little in her seat. "Starla's certainly a sweetheart, isn't she?"

Great. *Now* she decides to talk. When talking was the last thing he wanted to do. Being around Starla did that to him, never mind how annoyed he got for letting it—her—get to him. However, instead of taking his noncommittal grunt as her cue to drop the subject, Laurel said, "She reminds me a little of my mother. Although Mom would've been, let's see...sixty-one by now. Wow. There's a weird thought."

Tyler glanced over, frowning. "Would have been?"

"Yeah," she said on a sigh. But not one of those pouty, poor-me sounds that drove him nuts. "She died when I was eleven."

"Oh." He looked back out the windshield. "I'm sorry."

"It's okay, it was a long time ago. More than twenty years. Speaking of weird. They say time heals everything, but I'm not sure that's true. Wears down the sharp edges, maybe, so they don't hurt anymore. Or at least not as much..." She pressed her fingers to her lips. "And I'm rambling, sorry. Must be the sugar rush from the cookies."

"No problem." Since as long as she talked, he didn't have to. Or deal with the crazy thoughts swirling inside his head. But since she'd brought up the subject...

"And your dad...?"

She hesitated, then said flatly, "Heart attack when I was fifteen. But I didn't see him much, anyway, after my mother died."

Pain flashed, like stubbing an already-sore toe. "Why not?"

"Who knows? Wasn't as if we ever discussed it. Although my guess is that he couldn't see himself as a single father. Or any kind of father, frankly, since he'd never been real hands-on before."

He spared her a quick glance. "So where'd you end up living?"

"With my grandmother. My mom's mom."

"And was that…okay?"

"Actually it was the best thing that could have happened. I adored her, for one thing. And at least she wanted me. My father obviously didn't. And since my grandfather had died a year or so before, well…we kept each other from falling apart. I know Gran did me, anyway."

They stopped for a red light. "What a crappy thing to do to a kid. Your dad, I mean."

She was quiet for a moment, then said, "People are who they are. They don't change simply because you want them to." Her shoulders bumped. "So like I said, it worked out the way it was supposed to—"

Boomer started barking at some dog in the car next to them. Tyler reached around and yanked the mutt back from the window. "You don't own the street, dumbass *Hey!* Knock it off! Lay down!"

On a frustrated sigh, the dog obeyed. Only to *whumph-whumph* under his breath for the next several seconds, making Laurel chuckle.

"So is your grandmother still around?" Tyler asked as the light changed.

"Oh, yeah. You might've seen her. Tiny, white-haired? Drives a Prius?"

"That's your grandmother's?"

"Yep. She sold her house a few months ago and moved to Sunridge—"

"The retirement community over by the outlet mall?"

"The very one. You ever been there?" When he shook his head, she chuckled. "I swear, if the age limit wasn't fifty-five, *I'd* be tempted to move in. Gran says it's to prepare everyone for heaven, since it's highly doubtful it could be much better than Sunridge. Anyway…so that's when I bought the house."

"Wait—you'd been living with your grandmother all that time?"

"Oh, I was away for a few years, during college, and then after, when I lived in the city. Then I moved back," she said without a trace of shame in her voice. "One, because I couldn't stand the thought of her being alone as she got older, and, two, because staying there let me sock away a nice chunk of change for my down payment. Between that and the low interest rate I got on my mortgage, my payments are like nothing."

"But wasn't that a little hard on, um, your personal life?" At her silence, he sighed. "And I just stepped way over the line, didn't I?"

Another light laugh preceded, "That's assuming I have one."

"A line? Or a personal life?"

"Either. Both. Although Gran always made it clear my life was my own. Well, within reason, of course. And not until I'd reached what she called the 'age of reason.' But she always encouraged me to make my own choices, to do what feels right for me, without worrying about what anyone else thinks of those choices. So it was my choice to move back to Jersey, to stay with Gran as long as she wanted me around."

"Then she moved out on *you*."

"Pretty much. Said I was cramping *her* style. But we still see each other at least once a week. She's my rock," she said softly, then smiled. "Even if she does drive me nuts on a regular basis. And it sure beats talking to myself all the time."

"You don't date? Go out?" She gave him another look, her mouth twitching at the corners. "Hey. You're the one who said there's no line. So I'm curious why you're always home. Since you seem really nice," he pushed on. Because he was an idiot, for one thing, and it wasn't like he ever intended to make a move on the woman, for another. "And you're okay looking—"

She laughed again. "So much for thinking you were one of those charmer types."

"And you've got a really nice laugh—"

"Dude. *Awesome* last-minute save."

"Not to mention a pretty decent sense of humor."

"Why, thank you."

"You're welcome." He paused. "You think I'm a charmer?"

"I've seen you with your lady friends. From time to time. So, yeah. You definitely know how to work it."

"You've been spying on me?"

"Says the man who wonders why I'm always home."

"Touché." They turned back down their street. Sensing they were almost home, Boomer plopped his drooly chin on Tyler's shoulder, whining softly. "Still. You make it sound like your grandmother's the only person you ever see. Which—no offence to your grandmother, I'm sure she's a great lady—but—"

"I *like* being alone," Laurel said quietly. "Not all the time, no, but…*alone* is my safe place. Really. Besides which, I'm a writer. I don't go out much because I work from home. And my girlfriends—from school, from when I worked in the city—they've all moved on. Or moved away. They got married, started families… I mean, sure, we all meant to keep in touch, but then everyone got busy, and…" As they pulled into Tyler's driveway, she shrugged. "That's life, right?"

Not sure what to say to that, Tyler mumbled a noncommittal "I guess," then got out of the car, herding the dog back inside the house and quickly shutting the door. Much offended howling ensued.

"Puppy's not happy?" Laurel said when he returned.

"What was your first clue?" he said, backing out of the driveway again. "And he usually goes with me wherever, but I don't know if I can take him in with us at the brick-yard, and I don't like leaving him in the truck."

"I don't blame you," she said. "So I take it you've known Starla for a while?"

"Jeez, lady—signal before you turn, okay?"

"Sorry, got tired of talking about myself. Another haz-ard of living alone, you forget the finer points of human interaction. And being a novelist, curiosity is my default mode. Relationships fascinate me. *People* fascinate me."

"You think I'm fascinating?"

"I was talking about Starla?"

"Oh. Right."

"I'd love to know her history. What, or who, made her who she is today. It's like...her past *shimmers* through her. Don't you think?"

He had to laugh, even though the conversation was mak-ing his chest ache. "You got this from like five seconds?"

"Well, it does. And anyway, I pretty much think that about everyone I meet. I love people."

"Just not being around them?"

Now she laughed. "Guess that does sound a little weird, huh? But as I said, she reminds me a little of my mother. That whole free spirit thing she's got going on. Love it. Especially since I'm so not a free spirit."

"Judging from this conversation? Don't underestimate yourself. And didn't you say you live life exactly the way you want to? How much freer could you be?"

"That doesn't mean I don't like structure. Or order. I'm

a bit of a neat freak, actually. In fact, sometimes I think that's why I like living by myself, because I'm sure I'd drive someone else nuts." She wrinkled her nose. "God knows I did Gran."

An image flashed through Tyler's head, of his own house. A neat freak, he wasn't. "So I'm guessing you're not a risk taker?"

He'd only meant to tease, to follow the lead Laurel had given him. So her stillness threw him, made him glance over at her. "Not generally, no," she said quietly, then offered him a slight smile. Facing front again, she nodded toward the brickyard's large sign about a half block away. "Is this it?"

"Uh...yeah."

Tyler pulled the pickup into the parking lot, inexplicably annoyed that Laurel didn't wait for him to come around and open the door for her. Even though there was no reason for her to wait. Or for him to play the chivalry card.

Same as there'd been no real reason for him to sidestep her completely innocent query about Starla. Other than habit. And self-protection. Which he supposed *was* the habit. He'd just never been keen on talking about stuff he hadn't worked through himself. Especially with strangers. He did wonder, however, as he grabbed the glass door to the showroom before Laurel could, whether she *realized* he'd dodged her question.

And why, even if she did, that should bother him.

The block yard blew Laurel's mind.

Mountains of the things, in a staggering number of colors, shapes and sizes, stretched before her like some ancient religious site. Oh, sure, she and Tyler had settled on brown, rather than prison gray, but what shade of brown? Light, dark, reddish, taupish...?

She jumped, knocking into Tyler when a forklift *beep-beeped* right behind her, then rumbled past them across the packed dirt field. He caught her long enough to steady her, to slightly rattle her…to remind her of their conversation in the truck coming over. The thrust and parry of it, the gentle, comfortable teasing—which she'd never experienced with any guy, ever—interspersed with the occasional avoidance. As in, Tyler's—

"You okay?" he asked, still gripping her shoulders.

Oh, my. "Sure."

Not that either of them owed the other anything, of course. Whatever he chose to tell her, or not, was his business. They were only here to buy blocks. To build a fence. So his dog wouldn't get loose anymore—

"So whaddya think of this one?"

Tyler had walked over to a display of the various offerings, centered by a largish, gurgling fountain, to point to a row of clay-colored blocks that actually looked…not terrible. "Sure—"

"Or…I dunno." Bending over, he rested his palm on one that was a lighter color, more beigey. Guy had a nice butt, she had to say. Well, think, anyway. "Maybe this?"

Laurel dislodged her eyeballs from his tush. "Which goes better with what you already have?"

He straightened, dusting his hands. "Either would work. You?"

"Same here. Price?"

"They're the same. But you know…" He slugged his fingers into his jeans' pockets. Which already sat kind of low. Then he looked at her with a little-boy grin that, when paired with the streaked, dirty-blond hair—not to mention the low-slung jeans—got all sorts of things fluttering and sighing and giggling. *How* old was she, again? "No reason we couldn't do both."

The baby stirred, jolting her back to reality. "Both?"

"Use two colors, make a pattern. Nothing weird or wild, just…not boring. It won't look stupid, I promise."

"Then…sure. Why not?"

More grinning. "Yeah?"

Honestly. The kid in the ice-cream store, getting to pick two different flavors for his ice-cream cone. Laurel laughed. "Yes. Because you're right. One color would be boring."

She laughed again when he did a quick fist-pump, then pulled a piece of paper from his back pocket he'd shown her earlier, with all the specifications already figured out. Fifteen minutes later, their order placed and delivery arranged, they were back in the truck, Tyler practically buzzing with excitement as he went on about how he'd demo the old fence that night, if it was okay with her, then get started digging the trench for the new wall so he could get on it by the weekend.

His enthusiasm, if not contagious, was definitely endearing. Except then he seemed to catch himself. "And you're not the least bit interested in any of this, are you?"

"In how this wall is going to happen? Not really. But I think it's terrific you are. Seeing as you're the one who's going to make it happen."

With a grin and a shrug, he looked back out the windshield. "I like…putting things together. Making the pieces fit. Even if it's only a wall. Because there's something really satisfying about building something from nothing, you know? No matter how long it takes, or how much you might swear in the process," he said, and Laurel chuckled.

"I can relate, believe it or not. Even though I'm working with words and ideas and not cement and blocks, it's sort of the same thing, isn't it?"

"I never thought about it like that, but…yeah. I guess so."

They rode in silence for a while until she said, "You know, that Green Day song you were playing earlier? I haven't heard it in forever. You mind putting it on again?"

Tyler frowned over at her. "You sure?"

"Absolutely."

A moment later, the cab was filled with sounds from Laurel's past, from a time when her future stretched out in front of her, ripe with promise. Not that it still didn't— the baby shifted again, bumping almost in time with the music—but boy, could her life *be* any more different than she'd imagined?

"Hey...you okay?" Tyler asked, which is when she realized her cheeks were wet.

Laurel dug in her purse for a tissue, wiped her eyes. Blew her nose. "I'm fine. This takes me back, that's all."

"To a better time?"

"To...a different one, maybe. But not better." She paused. "Or worse. And I have no idea why I'm reacting like this," she said with a little laugh. "It's only a song, for heaven's sake. And it's not like I don't listen to old music all the time. Music I have a connection with, even. Like the music my grandmother played—old jazz, Big Band. Perry Como," she said, chuckling. "But...that was her past, wasn't it? Her nostalgia? Not mine."

"I...guess?"

"Sorry. Another hazard of living alone, I spend way too much time in my own head. And it can get kind of creepy in there."

"Tell me about it," Tyler muttered as they pulled into her driveway. From his house, they could hear Boomer barking. "Dumb mutt recognizes the sound of my car."

"Which would make him not dumb at all. Confused, though, since it's in the wrong spot."

"You're probably right."

And that should have been where she got out of the truck, he switched from her driveway to his and that was that. A total nonevent.

Not their facing each other at the same moment and her saying, "Wanna get a hamburger or something? My treat."

The music stopped. The dog kept barking, barking, barking…

"Uh…it's only three o'clock?"

"Oh." Laurel mentally slapped herself. And not only for not knowing what time it was. "Of course, you're right. But tell that to this…my stomach."

"Actually," he said—very gently, like the way you talk to the crazy woman, "I gotta get back to work for a little bit—"

"Of course, sorry—"

"No, it's okay. Another time, though?"

"Sure, absolutely." She climbed out of the truck as gracefully as she could, which wasn't saying much, and shut the door.

Tyler leaned across the gearshift to talk to her through the open window. "But I'll still start taking down the fence this evening. You don't have to be around or anything. If the noise gets too loud, though, let me know—"

"I'll do that," she said, backing away, suddenly anxious to get back to her own safe little space, where she could coddle her embarrassment without witnesses. "Thanks. For everything."

With a little wave, he pulled out of her driveway, and Laurel mustered whatever vestige of dignity she had left to sedately walk across her yard and up her steps.

Instead of, you know, bolting like a freaked-out rabbit.

"Jeez, what's with the frowny face?"

With a grunt, Tyler walked past his sister Abigail, sitting

cross-legged on the dusty warehouse floor as she sanded flaking black paint off a late-nineteenth-century, wrought-iron chandelier, which she'd then refinish and slap up on eBay...and probably resell for ten times what they paid for it. Naturally, she got up and followed him to the office, a blond terrier in a ponytail and combat boots.

"So did you get the blocks and stuff for the wall?" He threw her a look. "I think that's called an opening gambit," Abby said, and he grunted again. "Oooh...frowns *and* grunts?" She planted her skinny butt on the crappy folding chair across from his equally crappy metal desk. This was a salvage company, not some chi-chi Manhattan office. "Intriguing. But God forbid you clue me in."

He caught the edge to her voice, tossed it aside. Whatever was going on inside his aching head—and right now, he couldn't explain it even if he wanted to—it was none of his sister's business.

"Back off, Abs," Ty said, reaching for a bottle of pain reliever in his desk. He dumped out a couple of pills, tossing them back without water. With a pushed-out sigh, Abs got to her feet; a moment later he heard the water cooler's *glug-glug* as she filled a paper cup.

"Here," she said, handing him the cup, which he drained.

"Anything of interest happen while I was gone?"

"Not really. Couple of lookie-loos. One couple redoing their house, though, looking for some vintage stuff. I think they'll be back." She paused, her gaze sharpening in a way that put Tyler on immediate alert. "The bank called."

Crap. "Oh?"

"Yeah." His sister crossed her arms over a paint-blotched T-shirt that emphasized how uncurvy she was. "Why didn't you tell me you tried to renegotiate the loan?"

Tyler sighed. "Meaning they said no, I take it."

"I don't know, they wouldn't tell me. Since you didn't include me from the get-go—"

"I was putting out feelers, Abs. That's all. To see if it was even feasible. I didn't sign anything, so it's not like I left your name off—"

"No, you just left me out. As usual. I thought we were supposed to be partners? I mean, are we having trouble making the payments? Not that I'd know, since when I tried to get into the accounting program, you'd changed the password."

Tyler frowned. "I changed that password a month ago. And I told you the new one. Which you obviously never tried to use."

Her mouth thinned. "Maybe I didn't think I needed to. Because I trusted you."

"Or because, as you've said countless times, you hate numbers."

"I hate going to the dentist, too, but I deal. And I have a right to know what's going on. Without having to look it up for myself in some cockamamie computer program that makes my eyes cross. Dammit, Ty—I've worked every bit as hard as you to get this place up and running! Invested every bit as much in it, too! Emotionally and financially!"

And those pain meds could kick in anytime now. "I know you have, honey. Which is why I didn't want to say anything until there was something *to* say. I didn't want to worry you—"

"Because…you didn't think I could handle it, what?"

"So sue me for wanting to protect you—"

"I don't need to be protected, I need to be included! And not only when it suits you, dumbbutt. But why am I wasting my breath? Since you never have, not really. Hell, none of you have—"

"What are you talking about?"

"You, Ethan, Matt, even Bree…it's like the four of you are all in this secret club or something, because you're all adopted and I'm not. *And* I'm the baby. So double whammy, right?"

Tyler almost laughed, which only got him more glaring from his sister. "If it makes you feel any better, we don't share much with each other, either. Except for maybe Sabrina and Matt, because they're twins. But the rest of us…" He shook his head. "Trust me, you're not missing out."

Breathing hard, Abby kept her gaze glued to his for several seconds, then marched back to the cooler to get her own cup of water, which she downed in three swallows. "You know what?" She crumpled the tiny paper cup, slam-dunking it into the garbage can by Ty's desk. "You're right," she said, sounding a little less steamed. "Because this whole family's a bunch of emotional retards, aren't we?"

"What?"

"No, it's true. We all talk *at* each other, but nobody talks *to* anybody. Not really. Well, I don't know about Matt, now that he's got Kelly and the kids, maybe he's loosened up a bit. I hope so, anyway, for their sakes." She sighed. "And I get it, that simply because we're family, that doesn't mean we're obligated to talk about our innermost feelings and all that crap. And I'm every bit as guilty of that as the rest of you. But…"

Planting her hands on the desk, Abby leaned forward. "*This* is supposed to be a partnership. So no more keeping secrets about the business, or I'm outta here." She straightened, her arms crossed. "Got that?"

Tyler kept his smile under wraps, that the toddler who used to follow him around like a puppy—when he was a hard-assed adolescent who definitely did not want some baby tagging along behind him—had turned into such a fierce little thing. He also knew her threat was a lot of hot air, because, like she'd said, she'd poured her heart and soul into making this venture work. Sometimes, even more than Tyler. So it would probably take a lot more than his occasionally keeping her in the dark to make her walk away. Piss her off, absolutely. But she wasn't going anywhere.

Any more than he was about to change how he did things. Not anytime soon, at least. Because as smart as Abs was, and as good an eye as she had—and as much as Tyler truly respected both of those things—his sister also had a bad habit of letting her feelings get the best of her... an indulgence Tyler hadn't allowed himself since the fourth grade. He had no problem with Abby giving her heart free rein as far as the esthetic side of things went. But the business end, the money end—for that, you needed a clear head. Focus. Not muddied emotions.

Because all emotions did was mess things up. Make you feel like you'd lost control. Not going back to those days, boy. Ever.

So, yeah—the nuts and bolts that kept this whole thing going, and from going under...that was his province. And he wasn't about to give it up. However...in the name of familial, not to mention workplace, peace, he supposed he could throw the glowering young woman in front of him a stick.

"Got it," he said, then picked up the phone, punching the conference call button. "Wanna listen in while I talk to the bank?"

After a moment, Abby nodded, then sat back down, apparently mollified, and Tyler released a long breath that took at least some of the headache with it.

Chapter Three

Seated at her kitchen table, Laurel grinned over her cup of tea as she watched her grandmother contort her eighty-five-year-old body to look out the kitchen window while she washed up the lunch dishes. At, it wasn't hard to guess, Tyler digging a trench for the wall.

"You do know I have a dishwasher, Gran, right?"

"And you do know he's taken his shirt off, right?"

"I do now."

Marian McKinney twisted to frown at Laurel over her shoulder. "And you don't want to come see?"

"Not particularly," Laurel said with the most nonchalant shrug she could manage. Tyler in a muscle-hugging T-shirt already left nothing to the imagination. Tyler *without* the T-shirt...

Yes, she—and her bouncing baby hormones—had gotten over whatever had sent her into a tizzy a few days ago. But still. Some things were best left unseen.

Or thought about.

"And you, Gran, are a dirty old lady."

Her grandmother swatted in her general direction, flinging water and Palmolive suds across the floor. She had a hot date later, apparently, so was all decked out in a bright purple pantsuit and the diamond studs Grampa had given her for her fiftieth birthday, her glistening white hair appropriately poufed for the occasion.

"I'll take dirty over dead any day, believe me."

"Does what's-his-name know this?"

"Thomas. And if he doesn't—" she turned, her pale blue eyes twinkling behind her trifocal lenses as she dried her hands on a dish towel "—he'll soon find out."

"You hussy."

"Damn straight," Gran said, neatly folding the towel before hanging it back up, then carrying her own tea over to sit for a few minutes before she left. Every Saturday, come hell or hurricane, they had lunch—a tradition they'd started when Lauren was in kindergarten, only broken during those years she lived in New York. This time was theirs…and Laurel wasn't sure which one enjoyed it more.

Despite Gran's oft-verbalized discomfort with Laurel's decision to be a single mother. Not because her grandmother was a prude—obviously—but because—

"What did you say his name was again?"

"Tyler. Noble."

Gran's forehead crinkled. "Noble, Noble…" She snapped her fingers. "One of Preston and Jeanne Noble's kids?"

"I have no idea. Who are Preston and Jeanne Noble?"

"He'd just retired from the air force when I met them, oh, way back. Before you came to live with me, when Harold was still alive. Jeanne and I were both working on some fund-raiser or other, Harold and I had dinner with her and the Colonel one evening." She laughed. "They spent the whole night talking about 'their' kids—they'd been fostering for a while by that point, but had adopted two or three as well, as I recall. Not as babies, either, as little kids. Wonderful people," Gran said on a sigh. "Especially her. I would have loved to have kept up with them, but then Harold got sick and…" She shrugged. "So wouldn't that be funny, if Tyler was one of theirs? I mean, he's such a nice young man…."

"Which you could tell after, what, twenty seconds when you took him a sandwich?"

"You'd be surprised how much you can tell in twenty seconds," she said, and what could Laurel say to that? "Especially when you get to be my age and can spot the BS within ten. And if he is one of the Colonel and Jeanne's brood—"

"Gran. Honestly."

"You could have at least invited him in to eat with us—"

"And I already told you, Ty said he only had a few hours to work. He has to go see a client later—"

"Oooh…*Ty*, is it?"

"For the love of Pete, Gran," Laurel said, laughing. "Give it a rest."

"But honey…it's so hard, raising a child on your own—"

"*You* managed."

"You weren't a newborn. *That* would've killed me."

"I somehow doubt that." Laurel got up to rinse out her cup, taking care to avert her eyes from the glorious, slightly sweaty sight twenty feet past the window. After stealing the quickest peek. Long enough to see him bopping his head as he measured, she presumed in time to whatever music was coming through his earbuds. Inwardly sighing, she turned back to her grandmother. "But it's not as if I'm a teenager, or penniless. Or homeless—"

"No. Just stubborn."

"Gee. Can't imagine who I got that from."

Gran's grimace bit into a face already deeply lined from too many summers spent on the shore when she was younger, and Laurel smiled. "Besides," she said gently, "Tyler's obviously younger than I am, and—"

"Oh, pish. Harold was six years younger than I was. No big deal."

Laurel's brows crashed. "I never knew that."

"Yeah, well, neither did he. Because I lied about my age," she said with a little "no biggee" flick of her hand. "It was easier to get away with back then. Nobody checked. And since I handled all the household stuff, he had no reason to ever find out. So thank God he went before I did, or that could have been really embarrassing. But anyway," she said on a huff of air, "Harold could keep up with me, if you get my drift. Until he got sick, anyway. Until then, however—" she did a coy little shoulder wiggle "—ooh-là-là."

"Except I'm not looking for ooh-là-là."

"Don't kid yourself, sweetheart," Gran said, getting to her feet and collecting the pink quilted Kate Spade bag Laurel'd given her for her eightieth birthday and which she was now never seen without. Thing was getting a little dingy, truth be told. "Everyone's looking for ooh-là-là." She nodded pointedly at Laurel's belly, the pooch still barely visible underneath her roomy—and fortuitously fashionable—top. "Even you, at one point. Obviously."

"And look how late it is!" Laurel said, ushering her grandmother toward the door. "If you don't leave now, you won't make your movie!"

Fully aware of Laurel's diversionary tactic, Gran chuckled. But at the front door, the older woman turned and grabbed Laurel's hand. "I can't help it…I worry about you, baby." Behind her silver-framed glasses, her eyes filled. "I always have."

"Then you need to stop," Laurel said gently. "I'm not that eleven-year-old girl anymore. And believe it or not—" she cupped a hand over The Bump "—I'm happy. Really."

"But not as happy as you *could* be."

Laurel leaned over to kiss her grandmother's cheek. "I'm fine. Really. Now go have fun with your gentleman friend and I'll talk to you later."

"You're incorrigible, you know that?"

"I learned from the best."

On another air-swat, Gran turned and descended the porch steps, still on her own steam but definitely more carefully these days. But there was nothing cautious about her sure handling of her brand-new Prius as she smartly steered away from the curb and down the street...even if the car's stereo was loud enough to hear even with the windows up. Billie Holiday, sing your heart out.

Shaking her head, Laurel went back inside, where her laptop glared balefully from her coffee table. Swatting at it much like her grandmother had at her, she walked back into the kitchen. To...put the washed dishes away, that was it. And if her gaze happened to drift out the window...well. Gaze-drifting happened.

Her cell phone rang, startling the bejesus out of her.

"Hey," Tyler said. "Your grandmother still there?"

"No, she just left—"

"Got a sec, then? Cause I need you to make a design decision."

"Seriously?"

"You're gonna see far more of this wall than I am, so get out here and tell me how you want this pattern to go."

Laurel shoved her bare feet into a pair of leather flip-flops by the patio door, grabbed a bottle of tea out of the fridge, then went out onto the high-railed deck, mostly in shade this time of day thanks to the thirty-foot sycamore planted smack in the center of the yard. Next summer, she could put a portacrib out here, she thought with a little smile, where the wee one could nap while she wrote....

Tyler turned, grinning and sweaty and glistening, and she actually gulped. So wrong. Because, really, how old was this guy? Twenty-five, twenty-six...?

"Looking good," she said, then blushed. "The trench, I mean." Since that's all there was, at this point. Still grinning, the goofball shook his head, clearly finding amusement in her discomfiture. She held up the tea. "Thirsty?"

"That looks amazing. Yes."

Laurel skipped down the deck's stairs—something she probably wouldn't be able to do for much longer—and crossed the small yard, the cool, too-long grass tickling the sides of her feet. Since she still hadn't mowed. But the idea that she *could* mow her *own* yard...the thought still made her a little giddy.

She handed Tyler the tea, watching the muscles in his damp neck stretch as he tilted his head back, rhythmically pulse as he swallowed. Suddenly not feeling too steady on her pins, she sank onto the bench of her grandmother's old redwood picnic table a few feet away, grateful for the cool breeze meandering through the leaf-dappled sunlight. Tyler joined her to set the half-drunk tea on the table, then reached behind them for the tablet hidden underneath his rumpled, abandoned T-shirt, and Laurel thought, *Whoa.* Because, although the bloodhound sense of smell had diminished somewhat after the first trimester, thank God, after a couple hours spent working in the hot sun, the man's pheromones were singing like the chorus in a Verdi opera.

And she did love her some Italian opera, boy.

"Man, that feels good," he said, shutting his eyes for a moment as another breeze drifted through. Opening his eyes again, he picked up the T-shirt and swiped it across his chest, and Laurel nearly passed out.

"Nice yard," he said. "Was it like this when you moved in?"

Yard, okay. That, she could talk about. "The bones were there, but it'd been badly neglected. And of course I moved in during the Winter That Would Not End. Every time I thought I'd get out and start puttering, it'd snow—"

Or she'd feel like the walking dead, tossing her cookies every morning.

"—but now that Mother Nature's finally stopped with the schitzo routine, I've been working on it, little by little, to make it my own. Well, to make it look more like my grandmother's yard, which I loved. Hers was bigger, though. Much bigger. This is just right, though. For me."

"Your grandmother's something else, isn't she?"

"That's one way of putting it." She grinned. "You better watch out—she likes you."

"I know, older women can't keep their hands off me," he said, grinning back. "It's a curse."

"I'll bet," Laurel said, inwardly sighing as Tyler handed her the tablet and she got another whiff of hot, damp male. One who did not—thank you, Jesus—douse himself in man-stink cologne.

"I was playing around with some design ideas last night, this is what I came up with. But nothing's set in stone," he said, then groaned at his own lame joke.

She chuckled then forced her attention to the designs on the screen. "I think…this," she said, pointing to the top one, all one color except for two rows near the top, where the dark and light blocks alternated, checkerboard style.

"Yeah? Me, too. And you know what else would be really cool, right over there?" Leaning his elbows on the table, Tyler nodded toward the middle of the wall. "A fountain. Like you'd see in an Italian garden. Or English, maybe." He grinned at her, his mouth adorably lopsided, his hair adorably messy. She *could* say the feelings surging inside her were more of a maternal nature, but she'd be lying. "You know, where the water's coming out of the lion's mouth or something?"

"And where would I get one of those?"

"Actually there's one at the shop—"

"Of course there is."

"No, hear me out. It was part of a huge haul from a property over in Weehawken, from like a year ago. If you like it, I'll let you have it for really cheap." He winked, and she laughed—because the flirting, it was absurd, really—before, with another smile, he reclaimed the tablet. "Here, let me show you…" He scrolled through his photos, then turned the screen back around.

"Oh, my. That's quite lovely, isn't it?"

"I know, right? And it would look perfect there, with some rosebushes and sh—stuff planted around it. You can't really tell much from the picture, though, you should really see it in person. If you're interested, I mean."

"Well…I suppose that depends on the price?"

"Like I said, it was part of a huge haul, we're already in the black with it. So…twenty bucks?"

"You can't be serious?"

"Too high? Fifteen?"

"No! Tyler! For heaven's sake…you can't tell me you'd normally price something like that so low. Why on earth would you basically give it to me?"

He got quiet, then said, "It's a really cool piece, for sure—at least, I think so—but to be honest, it *looks* like it's a hundred-plus years old. Part of the lion's nose is missing, and it's got a lot of dings and cracks. It works fine, but it's not…perfect."

"But isn't that what gives it character?"

"You would think so, yeah. And it's not like we haven't sold stuff in worse shape. *Far* worse shape. I don't know why this guy hasn't moved. Unless…" He looked at her from underneath his shaggy hair. "Unless he was waiting for his right home."

"And you think my wall is it?"

"Could be," he said with a shrug—and another wink—before getting up again, grabbing the tea to finish it off. Laurel sighed.

"What?" he said, twisting the cap back on.

"Are you even *aware* you're flirting with me?"

He actually blushed. "Sorry, I… No. I mean, that's just me." Which was exactly what she'd thought. "Didn't mean to offend you or anything—"

"Oh, I'm not offended at all. Amused, perhaps. And I *was* going to say flattered." She sighed. "Until you made it clear it's not personal."

"It's not. I mean…please don't take this the wrong way, but—"

Yes, that was the story of her life, wasn't it? And again, exactly as she'd figured. "S'okay, I totally get it. Really. But you might want to pull back on the flirting thing. Because someday, somebody *is* going to take it the wrong way. And that wouldn't be good."

"No, ma'am, it sure wouldn't."

Thirty-five, and already ma'amed. So sad.

"So. Anyway," he said, "I'll get the footing poured tomorrow. Once that's set I can start building the wall in the evenings. I don't intend for it to take too long, though—I miss my dog too much."

"Oh, that's right—where is Boomer?"

"At my brother's. Matt's Newfoundland and Boomer are best buds—"

"A Newfie? Wow."

"Wow, is right. Alf's paw's about the same size as Boomer's head."

Laurel stood as well, the breeze messing with her loose top. "So you have a brother?" At Tyler's puzzled frown, she smiled. "I'm an only. The idea of siblings always intrigued me."

With a slight snort, Tyler grabbed the shirt, yanked it over his head. "Actually, I've got two. And two sisters."

"Seriously? Kudos to your mom." Little Bits started up with his jazz routine, but Laurel stopped herself from laying a hand over her tummy. Even though she had no idea why, it wasn't as if this was a secret. "That's a lot of babies to push out."

"Actually, she didn't. Except for Abby, the youngest, the rest of us were adopted. And there was always the occasional foster, too—"

"So your family *is* the one Gran was talking about!"

"Excuse me?"

"When I told her your name, she wondered if your dad was Preston Noble."

"That's him, yeah. He—they—adopted me when I was ten."

"She remembered briefly meeting him and your mom, when my grandfather was still alive. So, years ago. How are they?"

"Pop's doing okay, I guess. But Mom...she passed away several years ago."

"Oh...I'm so sorry."

"Yeah, it was rough on the old man. And Abs, she was only fourteen, fifteen, something like that." He paused then said quietly, "It's rough, losing your mother when you're still a kid. Which I guess you know all about, huh?"

"Yeah."

He picked up the tablet, tucking it to his side. "Mom was great," he said softly. "Not that the Colonel wasn't—isn't—but she was more about going with the flow. Pop's…he's a good man, don't get me wrong, but he had pretty definite ideas about how things should be done—" His phone buzzed. He pulled it out of his pocket, frowned. "Damn, it's later than I thought. I really need to go—"

"No, it's okay. I didn't mean to keep you."

"Look, I meant it, about wanting you to come see that fountain. Make sure you really like it before I lug it over here. Whenever you want… Here." He dug in the same pocket for a business card. "If I'm not there, Abs will be. So. Deal?"

"Deal," Laurel said, and he smiled. Like, right into her eyes, smiled. Then he hopped over the trench and up on his own deck before she finally hauled herself onto hers and back inside, where she turned on the central air the previous owners had installed, bless their hot little hearts.

Unbuttoning her blouse, she stood in the middle of the living room, where cool air washed over her bare, bulging belly. Not as much as some bellies bulged at five months, perhaps, but she definitely no longer looked as though she'd just gone on a doughnut binge.

As in, soon people would start noticing.

Like, say, hunky neighbors and such.

Hunky neighbors who were surprisingly easy to talk to, given how uneasy and tongue-tied and awkward she usually felt around men.

Not bothering to button her top—like who was gonna see?—Laurel returned to the kitchen for her own bottle of tea, reminding herself that even if she hadn't been pregnant, Tyler and she would have never happened. For a whole slew of reasons, spoken, unspoken, sort-of spoken…whatever. That, frankly, as sweet a kid as he was—and as much as her libido was letting her fantasies run amok—compared with her, he *was* a kid. And she hadn't been a kid since... well, ever, really.

She twisted off the cap, took a long swallow, then rubbed the cold, smooth bottle to her overheated forehead. Because for too many years—and except for one single, if major, lapse of judgment—she'd been about what made sense. What was practical.

Which Tyler Noble was definitely not.

On her return to her living room, her laptop once more caught her eye. She should really try to get at least a couple pages done today. Except, you know what? Her deadline wasn't for another month. And last week the words had flowed quite nicely, thank you. So if all went well she'd get the next book in well before the baby came, and then...

And then, she thought on a sharp intake of air.

Her life would change forever.

A little freaked, truth be told, Laurel plopped on her sofa and grabbed the remote, clicking through the menu until she found, of all things, a cooking show. Since, if she was going to be somebody's mother, she should probably learn how to feed the kid.

Because that was the practical thing to do.

Judging from the sounds and scents when Ty stopped by his brother Matt's after work to pick up the beast, everybody was in the backyard, where Matt's fiancée's kids rushed him and both dogs serenaded him like they'd been apart for years.

In front of the grill, Matt was tending enough burgers to feed all of Maple River. Boomer duly acknowledged and reassured, Ty scooped Aislin, Kelly's curly-headed three-year-old, into his arms and marched over, his stomach rumbling and his head fizzing a little, like it always did when he was around kids. Especially cuties like this one.

"Weren't expecting you 'til later," Matt said, flipping the sizzling meat and sending a plume of cow-scented smoke wafting into the humid, early-evening air. "Thought you had a date."

"She canceled," he said. Matt gave him a look; Ty shrugged. "It was pretty much done, anyway." His older brother gave a low chuckle. "What?"

"Nothing. You wanna stay for dinner? Kelly made potato salad that'll make you weep, no lie. And some ridiculous dessert." Ty's future sister-in-law was a caterer. Damn good one, too. "Seriously, if you don't help us eat this stuff, I'm not gonna fit in my uniform anymore."

"Can't stay. Since, now that I'm free—"

"Again. Or is that still?"

Tyler ignored him. "I might as well start on the wall. And you're a detective, when was the last time you wore a uniform?"

"Whatever—"

"Hey, Uncle Ty!" Tyler grinned over as Cooper, Kelly's eight-year-old son sprinted across the grass, the late-day sun glinting off his glasses, his warm brown curls. Ty gave the kid a high five.

"How's it goin', dude?"

"Great! Dad said he's gonna set up one of those big swimming pools, right over there!" He pointed to the far corner of the yard, where the Boomer and Alf were noisily wrestling. "Cool, huh?"

"Very cool," Ty said, shooting his brother a glance. Then, to Coop again: "You can swim?"

"Not yet, but Dad signed Linnie and me up at the Y for lessons—"

"Hey, sport, these are almost done. Go see if your mom's got the rest of the food ready."

"On it!"

Linnie squealed to get down; Ty obliged, watching the kids bound off before turning back to his brother. *"Dad?"* he said, shoving aside the strangest twinge of…something.

Underneath a dark beard haze that passed five-o'clock shadow at least three days ago, Matt grinned. "It just popped out the other day. Not sure which of us was more surprised."

"I can imagine. How's it feel?"

His brother lowered the lid on the grill, then crossed his arms. "Amazing? Scary? Humbling, for sure." Matt glanced toward the house. "I only hope I don't screw it up."

Like Tyler, Matt—and his twin sister, Sabrina, who lived in Manhattan—had been adopted when they were older, in their case after their parents died in a car crash. And, since Matt never mentioned his father, Ty suspected there were some unresolved issues there. True, they'd only been six when their folks died, but some things imprint early. He should know.

"Screw it up? Are you kidding? You've so got this, man." Ty clapped his brother's shoulder. "Seriously."

Matt sighed, but through a crooked smile. Dude was the happiest Ty had ever seen him. After his skank ex had cheated on him like that? On somebody who, as far as Ty knew, had never done anything wrong in his entire freaking life? He totally deserved to be happy—

"So you ready for the wedding?" Matt asked.

"Hey. All I have to do is show up." He snatched a piece of American cheese off the plate by the grill. "You're the one getting married. *Again.*"

"Your time will come, buddy. Yes, it will, don't give me

that look. You *sure* you don't want to stay for dinner? Or
you just gonna eat all my cheese?"

"Don't hold your breath, no, and don't get your boxers
in a bunch, there's still four pieces left. Okay, three," he
said, stuffing another slice in his mouth.

"Why aren't you staying?" Kelly appeared like an appa-
rition, setting a bowl of creamy potato salad flecked with
bits of red and green something or other on the tempered
glass table beside him.

"The wall," he said, trying not to drool, and she nodded.

"Right. Forgot. Then at least let me send home a dog-
gie bag—"

"You don't have to do that…"

"No arguments. There's plenty. And if you stare any
harder at the potato salad you're going to meld with it.
Coop, honey? Go get… Oh, never mind, I'll do it." She
patted Ty's shoulder. "Do not move."

After she tromped off, her red curls bouncing between
her shoulder blades, Matt chuckled. "The woman lives to
feed people. I am so blessed."

It was true, Ty thought later, as, laden with enough rations to see him through next winter, he parked in his driveway, Boomer panting his head off behind him. His brother
had been blessed, in ways Matt probably couldn't have
imagined a few months ago. But then, he'd always wanted
a family. Kids. And Ty had no doubt his big brother, who
used to keep an eye on all of them like a frickin' sheep dog,
would make a damn good father. Ty, however…

The very thought made him shudder. Not that he wasn't
crazy about his nieces and nephews—their oldest brother,
Ethan, had four kids—but having his own? No way. As far
as that went—he shoved the dog's head out of the bag of
food, grabbed it and got out of the car—he definitely knew
who he was. Or, in this case, wasn't—

"Boomer! What the hell? Get over here!"

Halfway to Laurel's, the dog stopped in his tracks, turned around. But only to plant his butt in the grass, then look over his shoulder. Then again at Tyler, all jowly pleading. In the distance, thunder rumbled from black-as-soot clouds, threatening another storm. So much for working outside tonight. Although, truth be told, by the time he finished eating it'd probably be too dark—and he'd be too wiped out—to get much done, anyway.

Then, faintly, even over Laurel's rumbling air conditioner unit and another round of thunder, Tyler heard music. Not clearly enough to make out what it was, even when he went closer—to get his mule-headed dog—but definitely not punk rock.

He grabbed the dog's collar and marched him back to the house and up the steps…where he looked over at Laurel's prissy little house, which sat more forward on the lot than his did. Meaning he could see in her side window pretty good. She had a lamp on, her back to him as she worked at her computer. She'd bunched her hair into a pair of ridiculous-looking ponytails sticking out on either side of her head…and she was swaying to the music. Like, from the depths of her soul.

And…singing?

She stretched out her arms, her head falling back… Yep. Singing.

He laughed out loud.

And Boomer whined, straining to break free of Ty's grasp. He looked at those pitiful yellow eyes, that even more pitiful underbite…and Kelly had hooked him up with so much food, he'd never be able to eat it all…

This, he could share. In fact, it would be wrong not to.

Phone in hand, he scrolled through his contacts and pressed Send, smiling when he saw Laurel jump. She fumbled for her phone beside the laptop, but he couldn't see her expression when she checked the display.

"Ty? What—?"

"You eat yet?"

She paused, still staring at her computer screen. "Why?"

"Turn around."

"Excuse me?"

"Just do it."

She did, gasping a little when she saw him watching her. The phone still to her ear, she got up, came to the window. Opened it. Now he could hear the music, some kind of jazz. Sultry. Blood-stirring. Was she wearing...pajamas? Hard to tell behind the screen.

"What *are* you doing?"

Pocketing his phone, Tyler held up the bag. A rain-scented breeze skirted across the porch, messing with his hair. "Inviting you to share a feast. And you can put down the phone now."

"Oh. Right." She did. "What kind of feast?"

"Burgers. Potato salad. Regular salad with homemade ranch dressing. And some dessert that defies description."

"Where did you—?"

"From my brother and sister-in-law. Well, soon to be. In a month. She's a caterer. As in, her cooking kicks *butt*. You do not want to pass this up, believe me."

Laurel lifted her hand to the back of her neck. Apparently felt the ponytails. "I'm already in my jammies," she said, yanking out first one, then the other, band. She ruffled her hair. To make it lay down again, he supposed. Didn't work.

"So I see," he said. "You do realize it's only seven-thirty?"

"Since I wasn't expecting company, what's it to you?"

He grinned. "Should I put mine on, too?"

"Let me guess. You don't wear any."

"You spoiled the surprise," he said, and she laughed. "So. You want to help Boomer and me eat this stuff or not?"

"Do I have to get dressed?"

"Not on my account. Do I have to stay dressed?"

"Yes."

"Party pooper," he said, and she laughed again.

"Bring the dog. We'll eat outside!"

Laurel'd eaten dinner already, of course. Hours ago. But the budding baby carnivore in her womb leaped at the prospect of hamburgers. And potato salad. As long as the salad was fresh and the hamburgers well-done. Because she wasn't taking any chances.

As if she hadn't done that already, she thought, ramming a comb through her sticky-outty hair. And was doing it again, since simply letting Tyler come over was a challenge to what little was left of her hormone-ravaged sanity.

She tossed a lightweight robe on over the pajamas, a set of her grandfather's she found while packing up Gran's house. Silk, no less. Comfy as hell. And roomy enough to hide an elephant in. Or, in this case, her little passenger.

The doorbell rang. The loose robe flapping around her thighs, she tramped barefoot through the house and opened the door, bending to get kisses from Boomer before grinning up at Tyler. All nonchalant and stuff.

"I thought the deal was, you were supposed to build the wall and *I'd* supply the food?"

"And you still can. Just not tonight." He came in, handing her the bag. "You sure about outside? Sounds like a storm's coming in."

"Not here yet, is it?"

"True."

She carried the food to her kitchen, Boomer keeping

her company as she emptied the bag of its carefully packed goodies—still-warm burgers swaddled in heavy-duty foil, the salads in plastic containers inside a thermal lunch box. With an ice pack. Laurel smiled: Whoever this chick was, she already liked her.

"Nice place," Tyler called from the living room.

"Isn't it exactly like yours?"

"Not even remotely. I mean, your place actually looks like a grown-up lives here." He came to the door, leaning on the jamb with his thumbs tucked in his pockets. Grinning. Sexy as hell. "Although the colors are a little girlie for my taste."

"Well, since a girl lives here, it's all good. Let's see... I've got tea, milk or water to go with. Name your poison."

"No beer? Or even soda?"

"'Fraid not," she said. "Hate the taste of beer, and I stopped drinking soda years ago. Although...hang on..."

She opened the fridge, rummaging about for a moment until she found the half-drunk bottle of white wine, way in the back. She pulled it out, triumphant. "Ta-da!"

Tyler looked like he was trying not to laugh. "Really?"

"What?"

"A, white wine with burgers? And B, how old is that?"

"Okay, you might have a point. Or two."

He chuckled. "Tea's fine." He pushed away from the door and over to the counter, where he started opening containers, and she thought, *In another life...*

"Silverware's in that drawer right in front of you," Laurel said, pulling out another bottle of tea for Tyler, water for herself. "Paper plates in the cupboard above..."

A few minutes later, the storm having moved off to torment someone else, they were out on the deck, the setting sun beginning to tinge the quivering sycamore leaves an apricot gold. Laurel planted herself in one of the two wicker rockers she'd also taken off her grandmother's hands, while Ty took the other one, setting their food and drinks on a small wrought-iron table between them. Out on the lawn a pair of robins scampered in opposite directions, occasionally stopping, heads cocked, before jabbing their beaks into the grass for a juicy earthworm.

As ravenous as those birdies, Laurel unwrapped her burger, checking to make sure it was cooked through before biting into it. Tyler, who'd chomped down willy-nilly, frowned over at her.

"S'it okay?"

"Delicious," she said, chewing. "Thank you."

"Matt tends to cook 'em to death, sorry."

"No, it's fine. Really."

Tyler took a swig of his tea, then leaned back in his chair. "So…you said you were a writer?" Her mouth full, Laurel nodded. "What do you write?"

She swallowed, then grabbed a napkin to wipe ketchupy juice off her chin. "Young adult novels. For hire, though, not really my own stuff." At his frown, she smiled. "And… you have no idea what I'm talking about, do you?"

"Umm…I'm guessing somebody pays you to write books for them?"

"Pretty much, yeah. My publisher gives me the story-lines and I flesh them out. For a series aimed at tweens— nine- to twelve-year-old girls. The Hamilton High Good Luck Club. I'm guessing you've never heard of it?"

"Um…no. But I've got a fifteen-year-old niece… Maybe she has."

"Very possible. The series has been going for nearly twenty years now. But I've only been writing for it for five."

"Impressive."

"Not really," she said with a light laugh. "I write fast, and it pays fairly well. And I don't have to worry about—"

She caught herself. "Traffic. Or clothes." She plucked at her attire. "Or office gossip. In some ways, it's the best job in the world. For me, anyway."

"So you're cool with telling somebody else's stories?"

"Oh, I've had a couple of other things published. Made bupkiss with them. Love to write, not a big fan of starving. So for now, this is good. And does Boomer always stare like that?"

Because he was sitting in front of them, mouth open, drooling, his eyebrows twitching as he looked from one to the other.

"God, dog," Tyler said, "you are beyond pathetic. Go lay down!"

On a groan, the dog chuffed over to the railing and collapsed on the boards…but without taking his golden eyes off the burger in Laurel's hands.

"Oh, come on," Laurel said. "How can you say no to that face?"

Ty stuffed the last of his burger into his mouth, reached for his plate of salads. "*That face* is what got me into trouble to begin with."

"Trouble?"

"Yeah. Okay, so a couple years back, I was dating this girl who decided she wanted a dog. So she asks me to go to the pound with her, help her choose. I say, sure, whatever. And while she's looking at all these little rat dogs— you know, with those yippy little barks?—I turn around and see this *thing* sitting in his cage, just…watching me."

At that, Boomer lifted his head, his attention fixed on Tyler. Whose attention was every bit as fixed on the dog. Laurel smiled.

"He knows you're talking about him." Grunting, Tyler dispatched another bite of potato salad. "So what happened?"

"I looked away. Because the dog was creeping me out, staring at me like that. And those *teeth*." The dog cocked his head, and Laurel nearly choked on the bite in her mouth. "So anyway, the girl—Hannah—she picks out her dog, we do all the paperwork, and then we leave—"

"You *left* him there?" Ty looked at her, then tipped his tea bottle at the dog, and Laurel nodded. "Right. Sorry. Continue."

"*Any*way…so I take Hannah and the rat dog back to her house, and then I come home, and I can't get the damn dog's face out of my mind. That one, not hers. Hers, I forgot about the minute I dropped her off. But I'm thinking, I don't want a dog. Don't *need* a dog, don't want the responsibility, the pressure of having to keep something alive…" He blew out a breath. "But that *face*. Yeah," he said when Boomer heaved himself to his feet again and came over, his whole back end shimmying as he laid his chin in Tyler's lap. "*This* face," he said, cupping the saggy-jowled head in his hands. "Suckered me right in."

"So you went back and got him."

"Like the second they opened the next morning."

He straightened, giving the dog a playful slap on the rump. Boomer twisted around, his stubby little tail a blur as he play-growled, giving Ty the side-eye, and Laurel laughed. The dog butted Tyler's hand, asking for more, and Tyler lightly smacked him again, making the beast bark. Tyler grabbed him, putting him in a headlock to make him stop barking, kissing him between the ears when he'd calmed down.

"You're a good dog daddy," Laurel said.

"I do my best. Since that's the only kind of daddy I intend to be."

"Really? You don't want children some day?"

"Considering how much of a pain in the ass I was as

a kid?" His mouth screwed up on one side. "I can't even begin to imagine the karma if I had my own kids."

Laurel looked at him, biting her tongue to keep from saying something stupid like, "Aren't you a little young to be making decisions like that?" Because, really, who was she to say? Especially given her own experience?

And enough of this foolishness, she thought, calling the dog.

Boomer immediately switched loyalties, his head swinging around so fast his jowls jiggled. "Come here, baby," she said, and the dog trotted over, planting his quivering bum on the boards before she even told him to sit.

Tyler sighed. "You're gonna spoil him."

"Oh, and like you don't? Here you go, sweetie…"

She held out a piece of her burger, which the dog took so carefully, so gently, Laurel gasped. "Whoa. I'm impressed. Good job."

"Can't take any credit, I'm afraid. That's how he was when I got him. Begs like hell, but at least he's polite about it. Boomer, no, she doesn't want your slobbery old face in her lap. Or in *her* face. Boomer, for God's sake," he said, getting to his feet to grab the dog's collar, since by now he was slathering her face with kisses, and Laurel was helpless with laughter, and the harder she laughed the more the dog licked, until—laughing as well—Tyler yanked the dog off her.

"*Boundaries,* mutt, jeez." Then to her: "You okay?"

"I'm fine," she said, wiping tears from her eyes with one hand as she rearranged her rumpled pajamas with the other. "Really."

Except then she realized Tyler had gone stock-still, holding on to his dog as he stared at her lap. No…not her lap. Her belly.

Clearly shocked, his gaze met hers.

"Yes, I'm pregnant," she said, getting to her feet. "Are we ready for dessert?"

Chapter Four

His head spinning, Tyler followed Laurel into the kitchen, staring dumbly as she got down plates, yanked the silverware drawer open for forks.

"Why didn't you say something earlier?"

"Because...we hardly know each other? Because this has nothing to do with you? And anyway, it's not as if I'm trying to keep it a secret, not my fault if you didn't notice...." She opened the dessert box and gasped. "Ohmigod, this looks incredible. Do we even need forks—?"

"Forget the damn dessert, Laurel! This is important!"

Those cool blue eyes met his. "Agreed. But not to you. Or for you." She turned to lean one hip against the edge of the counter, crossing her arms over what he could now see was a definite bump. "Or did something happen between us and I missed it...?"

"No! I mean...no. It's just..." His hand shook a little when he streaked it through his hair. "It's a shock. That's all."

She'd cut a slice of the kuchen or whatever it was and dumped it on a plate, was now forking a bite into her mouth. "Tell me about it," she said softly as she chewed.

"So...this isn't one of those deals where you decided to have a baby on your own? Like you went to a sperm bank or something?"

"No," she said on a dry laugh.

"So where's the father?"

"Right now?" Not looking at him, she took another bite. "I have no idea."

"Does he even know?"

"Yes. Does he care? Not really."

"Dammit, the kid has the right to know who his, or her, father is—"

"Plenty of kids grow up with only one parent," she said, her gaze plowing into his. "For plenty of reasons. And do just fine."

"True, but—"

"I can take care of my kid, Tyler," she said, walking past him to return to the deck. She plopped down in the same chair, hooking one bare foot around the leg of a stool to haul it over. Her feet up, she shoved in another bite and sighed. "God, this is so good. You said your sister-in-law made this?"

Tyler dragged the other chair around to face her, dropped into it. "How can you sound like this is no big deal?"

She poked at the cake for a minute, then looked out over the yard, where fireflies began to flicker in the dusk. "Because if I let myself *think* about what a big deal this is, I'll freak out. Not an option. I have no choice but to hold it together. If you're not on board with that, you can leave." Her eyes briefly met his again before she took another bite. "I promise you, this little guy will know who his father is. That much is in my power. Whether he ever lays eyes on the man isn't. I knew he was starting a new job out of state, but not what. Or where. He even changed his cell phone number. And who has a landline these days?" She shrugged.

His chest tight, Tyler looked away, and Laurel sighed.

"He's in his late forties. His kids from his first marriage are grown, he's not interested in starting over. And I knew that, going in," she said, almost more to herself than Tyler. "In fact…" Her mouth twisted into a wry smile. "He'd said he'd been fixed. Showed me the paperwork, even."

"You're kidding?"

"You don't seriously think I was simply going to take his word for it, do you?"

"How…romantic."

"This wasn't about romance, it was about… Hell, I'm not sure anymore what it was about." She stabbed another piece of the dessert. "Other than something that would have ended eventually, anyway. Since, you know. New job. Out of state."

"And yet…" Tyler gestured toward her belly, and she sighed.

"I know. And believe me, I wasn't exactly thrilled, either. Not at first. Raising a child on my own was definitely not part of the Big Design for my life. But after the initial shock began to wear off, I realized…things rarely happen the way you envision them, right?"

"So you're going to keep the kid?"

Her plate empty, Laurel set it on the glass table, then looked at him, a slight smile curving her lips. "Besides my grandmother, I have no other family. Not that I communicate with, anyway. And I'm going to be thirty-six come August. This could well be my only shot at this. I'm also already *so* in love with this baby…" She glanced down, caressing her belly, then back at him. "So, yes, absolutely I'm going to keep him. I'm not going to say I'm not scared, or think this is going to be easy." The smile grew a little bigger. "But I am excited."

"But the father…"

"Hey, I did my part. Ball's in his court."

"Except you don't know where he is."

"Ah, but he knows where I am. Where we are. Since I found out right after I moved in." She cupped her belly again, and Tyler wondered how he'd missed it before. Of course, you don't always see what you're not looking for, either.

"Look," he said, "my brother's a cop, maybe he can help you track this dude down, make him realize…" When she shook her head, he blew out a sigh. "He has obligations, Laurel. Legal ones—"

"Well aware of that. I'm also very aware of how little obligation has to do with love." Boomer walked over and laid his head in her lap; smiling, she gently stroked his head. "My father married my mother because she was pregnant, because his parents—not my mother's—bullied him into it, to save face with their country club buddies. Meaning my parents only stayed together because of me. No, actually, they stayed together because of the choke hold my grandparents had over my father. And don't think I didn't know it."

She looked out into the yard again. "At least these days that stigma is more or less gone. People have kids without being married all the time. But I know what it's like, having someone around who doesn't want to be there. How it makes you feel…like a mistake that can never be fixed." Her gaze met Tyler's again. "I refuse to do that to my child. If Barry decides, at some point, he wants to be a part of his son's life, fine. But I would never, ever force the issue. You can't guilt someone into being a parent."

"But financially, at least—"

Laurel leaned over, covering his hand with her own. "Your concern is very sweet, but totally unnecessary. I'm okay. We're okay. Really. I'm in a much better position to take this on than a lot of women—or girls—who find themselves in this situation. And don't think I'm not grateful for that." She patted his hand. "Let it go, sweetie. This isn't your battle to fight."

True. But that didn't stop his racing heart. Or thoughts.

"So how far along…?"

"Beginning of October. Halfway there."

"A boy, you said?"

"Yeah." Her mouth curved. "Jonathon. Sounds good with Kent, no? I thought about Clark, but…it's been done."

Tyler smiled in spite of himself. "You feel okay?"

Laurel leaned her head against the cushioned chair, her eyes twinkling. "And what would you know about that?"

"My brother Ethan's wife—Merry—she was sick a lot with a couple of her pregnancies. Early on, anyway. She said that was pretty normal?"

"It's different for every woman. And every pregnancy. Other than eating everything in sight, I'm fine." Then she stood. "But I do get tired easily, so…"

"Right, sorry." Tyler rose and called the dog then let Laurel walk him to the front door, where he turned, seeing something in those blue eyes that nearly shorted out his brain. A…calmness, he thought. Or at least a resolve. Which went along with what he'd sensed earlier, about her knowing who she was. What she was about. Of course, he'd had no idea then she was pregnant. But now, seeing the way she'd come to terms with this huge shake-up in her life…

Was it weird, how much that turned him on?

His head spinning, he started down the steps, then turned back. "I'll be here pretty early, to get going on the wall. Before it gets too hot."

"Good idea. Oh! The food—"

"Nah, you keep it." He glanced at her belly, felt his face heat. "You two need it more than I do."

He was almost to the steps before she called out, "Hey—whatever happened to that girl? The one you were with when you found Boomer?"

He shrugged. "We broke up pretty much right after that. It wasn't working out. You know how that goes."

"But at least you got a great dog out of the deal. So serendipity, right?"

Tyler looked down at the mutt, sitting on one hip at the top of the steps and sniffing the night air. Doofus. "Right," he said, then took his dog—and his free-as-a-freaking-bird self, back to his messy, quiet, peaceful, house....

The following Monday, Laurel picked up her grandmother in her trusty old Volvo, duly admiring Gran's sparkly, Indian-print blouse and equally sparkly earrings before heading back to the highway and, eventually, to Ty's salvage warehouse. An estate sale hussy from way back, Gran had squealed with glee when Laurel invited her to go along. And now, strapped all snug in the passenger seat, she beamed like a little girl on her way to see Santa.

But not, apparently, for the reason Laurel expected.

"I cannot tell you how grateful I am to get away from that place," Gran said as they zoomed past the first of several shopping complexes anchored by a Walmart or Home Depot or Costco. "Honestly, all those old biddies do is complain about their aches and pains, or bitch about this or that relative."

"I thought you loved it there!"

"Oh, the facility is lovely. And the food's not bad. But the *people*. What a bunch of whiners. Seriously. So this is good," she said, her hands clamped around the top of the

Kate Spade. "*And* I get to see your hot-to-trot neighbor again. So, bonus."

Laurel stifled a laugh. "Gran, I don't think hot-to-trot means what you think it means."

"Hey, I read things. I keep up. I know exactly what it means."

Then Gran gave her a pointed look, and Laurel sighed.

"He does know I'm pregnant."

"So?"

"And have we not learned anything from our prior attempts to fix me up?" Laurel said, pulling onto the exit ramp. "And by *we,* I mean *you.*"

Red lips rosebudded before Gran sighed. Laurel glanced over, feeling bad. Sort of.

"Sorry," she said gently. "But you really do need to back off."

Gran nodded, then said, "You mind if *I* ogle, then? Because cute butts are in very short supply where I am."

"Knock yourself out. Just don't be obvious, 'kay?"

"'Kay."

The parking area—calling it a lot would be pushing it—was virtually deserted when they pulled in, save for a banged-up white Subaru that looked vaguely familiar. A big sign steered them around to the loading dock in back, where an open garage door served as an entrance...and Boomer as the receptionist. Although he'd been snoozing in a patch of sunshine, at Laurel's and her grandmother's approach he jumped to his feet and trotted over, a quivering, whining bundle of joy.

"Where's your human, boy?" Laurel asked, bending over for some of that slobbery loving. "Where's Tyler?"

"Not here," said the fresh-faced little blonde in overalls and work boots standing in the open entry. A little blonde

Laurel remembered seeing before, leaving Tyler's house early one morning. Ah. "Can I help you?"

"I'm Laurel. Ty's neighbor—?"

"Oh, yeah, he said you might be over. To look at the fountain, right? Come on around, it's out back with the other yard stuff. No, Boomer, you stay here. I'm Abby, by the way. Ty's sister."

Sister. Got it. "And this is my grandmother, Marian McKinney—"

"And aren't you the cutest thing going?" Gran said with something like a cackle. "You know, I think Edith Avery's got a grandson about your age—"

"Gran! For heaven's sake! Oh, my goodness…" Laurel stopped dead at the sight of all the fountains and statues and suchlike positioned helter-skelter around what *had* been the parking lot, once upon a time. "Where on earth do you guys get all this?"

"Demos, estate sales, landscape outfits going out of business…" The blonde shrugged. "People bring stuff to us, too. So here's the fountain," she said, leading them over to where the piece was propped up against a chain-link fence. A fence topped with barbed wire. And a surveillance camera—one of several, Laurel could now see as she glanced around.

"Is that it?" Gran said, coming closer.

Laurel returned her attention to the fountain, the lion with his chipped nose staring blindly out from the center of the ornately detailed back, the intricate pattern occasionally interrupted by more missing chunks. "Yes," she said, falling immediately and completely in love. "What do you think?"

"We had one a lot like this," Gran said, fingering the rim of the equally embellished bowl. "When I was a girl, in my parents' yard in Princeton. Not the same color, a little smaller, but...oh, my. Does this take me back."

Laurel wrapped her arm around Gran's shoulders, giving her a hug before reaching out to caress the lion's head. Then she softly gasped.

"Wait...it's marble?"

"Rosetta, yeah," Abby said. "Can you imagine what it must've looked like back in the day? You don't find carving like that much anymore. Of course, it's kind of banged up, which is probably why nobody wants it—"

"Because people are idiots," Gran said, and both Laurel and Abby laughed.

"And your brother is nuts," Laurel said, adding, at the girl's snort, "Even in this condition, it has to be worth a fortune—"

"And I told you," she heard behind her, "it's not worth anything if I can't sell the damn thing."

She turned to see Tyler, fingers tucked into his jeans pockets, his goofy-looking dog sitting all kittywampus beside him, tags jangling and dust poofing around him as the mutt scratched his floppy ear.

"From the picture, I assumed it was cast concrete. Not..." She turned back, her heart beating a little faster. "This."

"Well, it isn't. Of course, if you don't like it—"

"No, it's beautiful! In fact..." Shaded by a lone, straggly elm on the other side of the fence, the smooth stone was cool under her fingertips. "It's exquisite. Exactly as it is."

"Then what's the problem—?"

"Hey," Abby said to Gran, "how's about I show you around inside—?"

"You're on," Gran said, and the two of them hustled away, gabbing like old friends, Abby slapping her thigh to get the dog to follow them...leaving Laurel alone with a man who, standing there with a frown gouging his fore-head, was sending her poor, neglected hormones into a veritable tizzy. And that, boys and girls, was the *problem*.

Big-time.

Tyler crossed his arms, trying not to react to how pretty Laurel looked in her floaty red dress, her hair all shiny in the sunlight. He'd been watching for a while, taking in the scene—the little *ooh* sound she made when she first saw the piece, the way she hugged her grandmother—and for a second he'd been unable to breathe, let alone speak.

Then a breeze plastered the dress to the baby mound under it and he thought, *Yeah. Right.*

No.

"The problem is," she said, coming close enough for him to get a noseful of her perfume, "that I wouldn't feel right about accepting something this valuable. I'm sure the right person will come along who can pay you what it's worth—"

"You like it or not?"

"That's not the point—"

"Yes, it is. Well?"

"I already told you I do."

"Then it's yours. Hey," Tyler said when she started to protest again, "it's mine to do with what I like." He paused. "And if you take it, then maybe I can see it sometimes."

"So if you love it so much, why don't you put it on your side of the wall?"

"Have you seen my yard? It'd be like sending Queen Elizabeth to Walmart." When she chuckled, he said, "And don't give me any of that 'it's not practical' crap. Because life isn't only about being practical…sometimes it's about doing what makes you happy."

"And you think this fountain will make me happy?"

"Judging from the look on your face when you saw it?

I'm guessing, yeah. But giving it to you makes me happy, too."

"Because…?"

"It just does, don't think about it too hard. So you wanna see inside, long as you're here?"

After a moment, she nodded. "But I'm not saying yes to the fountain. Not yet, anyway."

Tyler bit back his smile. "No hurry."

Like he did every time he entered the warehouse, Tyler felt a warm little tingle—that, after a few pretty rocky years, he'd found something that worked, and worked for him, something he could be proud of. Something that was his. Well, his and the bank's. Except then he got another tingle, that hot *damn* if he hadn't renegotiated that loan to his and Abs's advantage, saving them a nice little chunk of change over the coming years—

"This is hugely impressive," Laurel said, glancing around, grit crunching underfoot on the cement floors as they passed a rack of dozens of old wood doors, ranging from basic to majestic, then mantels and fireplaces, window frames and even entire staircase railings in cherrywood, mahogany, maple. At the far end of the floor, they heard Abby's and her grandmother's muffled conversation, punctuated by occasional laughter. Laurel smiled.

"Gran's in heaven, in a place like this. And something tells me she and your sister are two peas in a pod. Did you and Abby collect all this stuff yourself?"

"Not all, no. We bought the business from somebody I'd known for a long time, so we started out with a good inventory. Guy needed to sell fast because he and his wife were moving out West to be with their kids, and they'd already bought a house, so Abs and I, we pounced on it. We have a crew that helps us strip properties, when we win a bid. And a bunch of part-timers who help man the shop."

They heard Laurel's grandmother exclaim about something. "Maybe your grandmother would like a job?"

Laurel blew a laugh through her nose. "And if you offered, she'd probably take you up on it. This is *such* a cool place," she said, stopping in front of shelves of bins holding all kinds of hardware, from drawer pulls to finials. She lifted her head and inhaled deeply. "I love the way it smells. Like history."

"That's dust," he said, and she laughed. But it was nice, that she'd said that, because he felt the same way. "Simply because something's a little banged up doesn't mean it's not worth anything. That it shouldn't get a second chance. You know?"

"I do," she said softly, then hissed in a breath as her hand went to her belly.

"You okay?"

"Just a foot. Or maybe an elbow. Hard to tell." Her eyes cut to his. "Want to feel?"

"No! I mean…thanks, but—"

"It's okay. Moms sometimes forget not everyone's as into their baby as they are. If at all."

It was probably the high ceilings making her voice sound so hollow—

"Ooh, I really like this light fixture," she said, skimming her fingers over a twenties-era brass coach lamp. "It would look so neat by my front door, don't you think? And no, I'm not fishing for you to give it to me, so don't even go there. How much?"

"Fifty. But it's no fun unless we haggle."

"You're on. *Ten.*"

"Sold," he said, and she smacked his arm. Then she dragged out her wallet and dug a pair of twenties from it. Then, laughing, she stuffed the money into his shirt pocket, palming it so he couldn't remove it. Okay, he *could* have, but he didn't. In no small part because all these little electric jolts were zigzagging over his skin where her hand made contact. The hell?

Laurel blinked, her cheeks going all rosy before she jerked her hand away, returned her wallet to her purse.

Feeling a little warm himself, Tyler picked up the fixture. "You wanna take this back with you, or let me bring it?"

"Oh. Bring it, I guess. You know somebody who could install it for me?"

"Yeah. Me." At her raised brows, he grinned. "You'd be surprised what I know how to do."

And, yep, she blushed again. And Tyler didn't even feel bad about that. She went back to digging in her bag— God alone knew for what—and he said—God alone knew why— "Would you like to come to my brother's wedding with me?"

She stopped, midrummage, her gaze zinging to his. "As in, your...date?"

"No! Well, yeah, sorta. I guess," he said, wondering when his mouth and his brain were gonna work out their differences and start communicating with each other. "Hell, I don't know. As a friend, how's that? It's gonna be this little backyard thing, really small, nothing fancy—"

"You don't have someone else you'd rather take?"

"No, actually."

"Why?"

"Why don't I have someone else—?"

"No. Well, that, too. But why do you want to take me?"

"I'm...kind of taking a break from dating, I guess. And that's all I'm gonna say about that. And I asked you because..." The lamp was heavier than he'd realized. Tyler started toward the back counter, where the cash register was. "Because you said you don't have much family, and

I've got family coming outta my ears. So I figured I'd share."

Behind him, Laurel sputtered a laugh. "You're crazy."

"This is not news," he said, hefting the fixture up onto the counter, then facing her. "But I think you'd really like Kelly. My sister-in-law to-be. And my sister Sabrina. They're about your age, come to think of it. And Kell's got two kids, so she's been…well. Where you are. Twice. And…and I think it wouldn't hurt, you knowing more people than the ones inside your books."

"What makes you think I don't?"

"Do you?"

Their gazes tangled for a long moment before she sighed. "Not really, no." The breeze from a big floor fan a few feet away snatched at her scent, bathing him in it as she hiked her purse strap up on her shoulder. "And your folks won't think it strange, you showing up with this pregnant, thirtysomething woman they've never met to this *really small,* family wedding?"

Tyler went behind the counter to grab a manila tag and pen. "As if," he said, scribbling her name on the tag, then threading the string around a bend in the fixture. "Growing up, I never knew from one night to the next who'd be at the dinner table. There were always extra kids, my brothers' and sisters' friends, sometimes fosters. So trust me, nobody's gonna think anything one way or the other. Although I have to warn you—we're really loud when we're all together."

Laurel laughed then said, "When did you say this was again?"

"Saturday, three weeks. So you'll go with?"

"Hmm…I'll have to change my lunch date with Gran—"

"Bring her, too. No, really—"

"Bring me to what?" her grandmother said, appearing

from behind a display of wrought-iron gates. Abby followed, lugging a pair of andirons that probably weighed as much as she did.

"My brother's wedding," Tyler said, and a bright smile lit up the old lady's face.

"Oooh, I haven't been to a wedding in years!" This, with a look in her granddaughter's direction. A look which Laurel apparently ignored. Until her grandmother poked her and said, "And maybe there's a bouquet to catch, sweetie. What?" she said to Abby's choking sound as she wrapped up the andirons. "I'm just saying…"

"Honestly, Gran," Laurel said on a soft laugh, and Tyler grinned. A grin that died a quick death when he met that blue gaze and realized, in the brief moment before she turned away, her eyes were wet.

Chapter Five

It wasn't every day the groom manned the grill at his own wedding, or the bride catered the rest of the luncheon. But, on her way back from yet another potty break, Laurel found the brand-new Mrs. Kelly Noble in her father-in-law's spacious, granite-and-cherrywood kitchen, barefoot in her simple white silk sheath dress, her thick, red curls skewered with what looked like chopsticks as she arranged shrimp and veggie kabobs on a platter. On the other side of the island, her tiny, brunette, also shoeless maid-of-honor—Matt's twin sister, Sabrina, Tyler had told her—hauled another tray out of the oven.

"These go in the chafing dish?"

"Yep," Kelly said, shoving her tortoiseshell-framed glasses back in place. "Ready in fifteen!"

Sabrina whisked the tray through the dining room, then the open French doors letting in the scents of honeysuckle and roses, of barbecuing steaks and chicken; the carefree shrieks of kids being chased by barking dogs; the muffled chatter of a dozen adults, pierced by an occasional burst of laughter. As a child, Laurel had always dreamed of the big church wedding and the gleaming white dress, a glittering reception with dancing and music into the wee hours. But what could be better, or more real, than this simple, lovely, joyful celebration of family...and love?

And if it hadn't been for the knot of stupid, pointless envy lodged in her throat—and her baby's head lodged at the base of her spine—it would've been perfect.

Kelly flashed her a smile that immediately softened the knot. "Come on in, pull up a seat!"

"I should probably get back out there—"

"Really? Where it's hot and noisy and crazy?"

There was that. Especially since *out there* was where Tyler was, watching her every move. Frowning. As though perhaps regretting his rash invitation three weeks ago, because now he was stuck with this pregnant woman and her octogenarian grandmother? The wall was done, the coach lamp installed—he'd even put up a side gate for her. What further reason did they have to hang out?

None that she could see.

All she really wanted to do was go home, where she could curl up around her growing baby and fantasize about a pair of strong hands—say, ones that built walls and installed light fixtures and roughhoused with his dog— massaging the kinks out of her back. But since Tyler had driven them over in Gran's car—and, since between the heat, her shoes and her aching back, she didn't see herself trekking five miles back to her house—she was stuck.

So she smiled at Kelly and said, "Need help?"

Swiping a stray curl off her forehead, the redhead snorted a laugh. "What I need is to have my head examined, agreeing to my husband's insanity. *'So what's the big deal?'"* she said, lowering her voice to imitate Matt's deep, Jersey accent. *"'It's just a party, right? Except one where we get hitched.'"*

"He really said that?"

"He really did. And at the time it made perfect sense. But I mean it, please, come on in." She chuckled. "Keep me from feeling sorry for myself."

An option that worked both ways. Because all those happy people…blech. Not that Kelly wasn't the happiest of the lot—as in, disgustingly blissful—but at least there was only one of her.

"Love your dress, by the way," Kelly said, with an approving nod.

"Thanks," Laurel said, skimming a hand over the floaty, blue-and-purple watercolor print she'd probably never wear again. She heaved herself onto a bar stool, reveling in both the cool air blowing through the vents and her back muscles relaxing as she watched Kelly pull bags of salad veggies from the fridge. "I can't cook worth squat, but I can slice, if you like."

"You're on." She handed her a paring knife, cutting board and bags of red pepper, cucumbers, fresh tomatoes. "And no, I do not care how you cut 'em up. I'm easy."

"You must be if you let your brother-in-law bring a perfect stranger to your wedding." The baby moved, making her tummy muscles tighten for a second. *"Two* perfect strangers."

"A word that does not exist in this family. And anyway, your grandmother knows the Colonel, so there you are."

"I think *knows* might be stretching it. She worked with his wife or something, a million years ago. And she met him once. Not exactly bosom buddies."

Her eyes sparkling behind her enormous glasses, Kelly put a finger to her twitching lips, then motioned for Laurel to follow her. They crept through the dining room to another set of French doors opening into the sunroom, where Laurel could hear her grandmother and Tyler's dad yammering away. The silver-haired, broad-shouldered Colonel—who redefined intimidating—chuckled at something her grandmother said, and Laurel's mouth sagged open.

Kelly gave her a thumbs-up then they both scurried back to the kitchen like a pair of kids caught eavesdropping on their parents.

"Holy crap," Laurel said.

"I know, right? Matt says the Colonel's never been the same after Jeanne—his wife—died a few years ago. Not that this is a surprise. She was such a neat lady, and he obviously adored her. I can only imagine how hard it's been for him. It's good to hear him laugh."

Over the pang—because, heck, yeah, she'd like to be adored, too—Laurel released a short laugh. "That's Gran's gift." She thought of how her grandmother had kept their spirits up, after her mother died, deliberately prodding their funny bones in order to break the mesmeric grief that could have so easily suffocated them both. Except then she remembered the "catch the bouquet" comment and sighed. "Although she can be a real pain in the patoot, too."

"And you love her to bits." Nodding, Laurel pressed a hand to her heart. Because everything her grandmother did or said—yes, even the irritating stuff—stemmed from love, she knew. The redhead smiled. "It's also nice to see Ty with someone who communicates in something other than giggles."

Laurel's cheeks warmed. "Oh, we're not *with* each other... We're just neighbors—"

"So he said. But still. The giggling thing?" Kelly shuddered, and Laurel softly laughed.

"I've witnessed the giggling, once or twice. Although not for a while... *Ouch, baby.*"

Kelly's eyes shot to Laurel's face. "What?"

"Oh, it's nothing. But I keep having these little... twinges."

"Down low or up high?"

"High." Laurel palmed the top of the mound. "Here. Like my belly keeps making a fist."

Kelly looked relieved. "Braxton Hicks. Annoying, but harmless. So when are you due?"

Laurel decided against mentioning the backache. Especially since, now that she was off her feet, it'd gone away. Mostly. Probably caused by the heels. Which she wasn't used to wearing in any case. "Beginning of October."

"Get out! For real? God, I was huge by six months with both of mine. With Aislin I thought for sure I was going to birth a hippo."

"Tell me about it. Especially since it's gotten hot."

"Yeah, summer pregnancies suck. I used to take cool baths at night... They seemed to help."

"Good idea, I'll try that." She watched Kelly make quick work of a pile of washed mushrooms, her rings flashing, and she shoved down another spurt of envy. And got busy with her own knife. "Congratulations, by the way. Matt seems like a really great guy."

Backhanding a stray curl off her forehead, Kelly grinned. "They all are, those Noble boys. The Colonel and Jeanne raised 'em right. But thanks. It's been a long time coming—"

"Only like twenty freaking *years,*" Sabrina said as she reappeared, plucking at the deep neckline of her bright blue, cleavage-enhancing dress. She grabbed a pair of un-used kabob skewers off the counter and, following her sister-in-law's lead, twisted up her long, dark hair, impaling it with the sticks. Add some dangling flowers and white makeup, they could do *The Mikado*. "Talk about a long learning curve."

Laurel chuckled. "Ty said you were sweet on each other when you were kids?"

Her makeshift updo wobbling, the brunette leaned over the counter and grabbed a slice of cucumber off the cutting board, the enormous diamond in her engagement ring nya-nyaing Laurel, too. Brother. "Except neither dumbass bothered to clue the other one in."

"And sometimes these things need time to ripen. Oh, come on," Kelly said at Sabrina's eye roll, "what could we have possibly done about it when we were kids? Matt and I didn't…fit each other then."

"Not like you do now, I imagine," Sabrina said with a wicked grin, ducking and shrieking when Kelly smacked her with a tea towel, and Lauren thought, *I miss this.* Oh, she cherished her solitude, for sure wasn't *lonely*…but it'd been a long time since she'd had a gal pal to shoot the breeze—or the bull—with. Gran was great, but…it wasn't the same.

"You know," Sabrina now said, frowning slightly as she chewed, "you look familiar. Were you at Hoover High?"

"I was. But a year ahead, I think—"

"And I moved away when I was sixteen," Kelly said as Sabrina's phone buzzed. "So at the most we would have only been there at the same time a year—"

The brunette snorted. "Chad. Needing to be rescued, probably." Laurel had only briefly spoken to Sabrina's fiancé, but her immediate impression was that he didn't quite know what to make of this boisterous, cobbled-together family he'd be marrying into. "Good thing our wedding's not till next summer, it'll take at least that long to break the poor guy in. You need me for anything else, Kell?"

"No, I think I'm good. Thanks."

Laurel couldn't quite read the expression on Kelly's face as she watched her sister-in-law leave, but with a small sigh Kelly crossed to the counter to pull a jug of virgin olive oil and a bottle of balsamic vinegar out of a canvas tote. "So is your nursery ready yet?"

Laurel pulled a face. "There's a room that will *be* a nursery, but…no. And yes, I know this kiddo's not gonna wait until I decide on a paint color. Or a crib. Or, well, anything else. I mean, I went to Babies "R" Us, but…holy crud. Three aisles in and I nearly had a panic attack."

"Sing it, honey. Not that I don't totally love that store, but Eighth Layer of Hell when you've got pregnancy pickle brain. Took me two hours to pick out a stroller… Oh, sweetie!"

The tears came out of nowhere. Like a freaking tsunami. Instantly Kelly was around the island, draping an arm around Laurel's shoulders and handing her a paper towel to blow her nose.

"I'm so sorry—"

"Hush," Kelly said, giving Laurel a quick squeeze. "Listen, when I was pregnant I'd go under at the sight of an empty toilet paper spindle."

Laurel snuffled a laugh, then dabbed the stiff towel underneath her eyes as Kelly let go to perch on the stool beside her. Then she sighed. "But I'm not—this isn't like me. At all." She blew her nose. And felt her bottom lip go quivery all over again. She made a sound that was part laugh, part groan. "God, what is *wrong* with me? It's like aliens have taken over my brain."

"No, just your uterus. And it will pass. I promise." Then Kelly gently said, "Tyler told me you're doing this on your own."

"Yeah," she said on a shaky breath. "And I'm so…"

She stopped. Not that Kelly didn't seem to be a genuinely caring person, but they'd known each other for like a nanosecond. And it was the woman's wedding day—

"Scared?"

"Try petrified."

Kelly smiled. "Then welcome to a very large club. Oh, I suppose there's a few überconfident mothers-to-be out there, but I don't know any of them. Or want to, frankly. And God knows I *wasn't* one of them." She patted Laurel's hand, then got up to drizzle olive oil, then vinegar, over the salad. "Is anyone giving you a shower?"

"I... No." She frowned. "I hadn't even thought about it—"

"Well, consider yourself showered," Kelly said, picking up a pair of salad servers to toss the greens. "We will go back to Babies "R" Us— Yes, I'm going with you, I can live vicariously—and you will set up a registry, and you will invite every woman you've ever known, thus guilting them into giving this kid a gift—"

"I can't do that!"

"You can, and you will." Kelly lowered her chin and gave her a hard look. "How many wedding and baby gifts have you been suckered into giving over the years?"

Laurel's mouth twisted. "A few."

"Then there you are. The universe's way of evening the score." She leaned forward. "And you need to let the world know you are *celebrating* this little person's arrival. Right?"

"When you put it that way..."

Kelly jabbed one of the servers at her. "So name the date. We'll do it here, it's absolutely stunning in the early fall, when Jeanne's roses get their second wind. I'll bring the food—"

"Wait." Laurel's eyes narrowed. "Did Tyler put you up to this?"

That got a laugh. "He's a guy. Guys do not think in terms of baby showers. I, however, do. And it's been a while since I've given one, so watch out." At Laurel's smile, Kelly's expression softened. "But since you brought up the subject... men also aren't very good about saying when they're concerned about someone. But I can tell Ty is, about you "

"Hey," Laurel heard behind her, and she stiffened. Speak of the devil. Ack. "Matt wants to know, what's the holdup?"

Figuring her face was probably a lovely shade of lobster by now, Laurel decided against turning around. Especially since she had no idea how to handle Kelly's little revelation about Tyler. And even less how to handle the potential fallout if he'd overheard.

"Sorry!" Kelly said brightly, palming the island to wiggle her bright blue pumps back on, then hauling the huge glass salad bowl into her arms. "Lost track of time! This was the last thing, so we're ready."

Then she skedaddled out of the kitchen...and Tyler plunked his butt on the stool Kelly had recently vacated, the longneck in his right hand dangling between his spread knees. Like his brothers, he was wearing khakis and a royal-blue polo shirt, open at the neck. Unlike them, he wore loafers without socks. And a frown underneath the floppy, streaked hair.

"You were crying?"

Laurel took the crumpled towel to her eyes again. "It's what pregnant ladies do. For no good reason, most of the time." She gave him a smile as she slid off the stool. Her back twinged again; she ignored it. "I'm fine."

"Then why'd you make that weird face—"

"What weird face?" Gran said, coming into the kitchen. She'd gone all out today, in some salmon-colored chiffon number that reeked of mothballs and the Reagan era. And rhinestone-studded gold flats.

"This one," Tyler said, imitating her. Gran's beady eyes zinged straight to Laurel's.

"What's going on? And don't you dare lie to me."

"Nothing," Laurel said, pressing her knuckles into her lower back. "But I probably shouldn't've worn these shoes, and it's hot and—"

"We should probably get you home," Tyler said, setting the bottle on the counter and sliding off the stool.

"Home, hell," Gran said. "Where's your cell phone, sweetheart? I'll call your doctor's service, have her meet us at St. Luke's. You know where that is?" she said to Tyler.

"Yeah, that's where I had my broken arm set—"

"You guys!" Laurel said, not sure whether to laugh or clobber somebody. "I'm way too early, this can't possibly be labor—"

"You ever been in labor before?" Gran asked.

"No, of course not—"

"Then how would you know? Yeah, that's what I thought. So where's your purse? Tyler, you want to bring the car around?"

"You got it, I'll meet you guys out there—"

"Excellent," Gran said as Tyler strode off. "So. Laurel? Purse?"

"And I told you—"

Her belly tightened again, so hard she couldn't breathe. Or move. Or, alas, finish her sentence. Well, crap.

Swallowing down a surge of panic, Laurel sagged against the stool, waiting out…whatever this was. No, no… this was so not happening. Not now—

"My bag's with yours, Gran," she whispered over her hammering heart. "On the bench by the front door."

Her grandmother fake-smacked her forehead. "Of

course, I'm an idiot, we'll get it on the way out. Come on, sweetheart," she said, and that's when Laurel saw, past Gran's bravado, her own fear reflected in the old woman's eyes. Tucking her withered hand around Laurel's arm, Gran guided her toward the front door, whispering, "It's going to be okay, doll baby, I promise."

The very same words she'd said, Laurel realized as she slid into the front seat beside Tyler, the night Laurel's father dropped her off right after her mother's funeral, promising he'd return for her soon....

"You think it'll be much longer before we know what's going on?" Laurel's grandmother said, looking toward the double doors behind which Laurel had been whisked more than an hour ago.

Tyler pocketed his phone after Kelly's worried call, wondering how it was he always seemed to be the one reassuring everyone these days. That used to fall to the woman he'd finally learned to call Mom, the woman who'd patiently shepherded him through his godawful teenage years. She'd know exactly what to say, he was sure. How to *be*.

Because, like pretty much everybody else on the planet, Tyler hated E.R. waiting rooms. That feeling of helplessness, the aroma of fear. The way his heart refused to settle down into anything even reasonably close to a normal rhythm. And right now, he especially hated the agitated expression on the old woman's face, her dress floating like koi fins as she paced with her arms tightly folded over her ribs, because there wasn't a damn thing he could do or say to ease her mind.

Or his, he thought, as remnants of years-old dread chugged through his veins.

Of course, this time wasn't anything like the night Jeanne collapsed, and it'd only been him and the Colonel in the house when the ambulance came. Tyler had driven Pop to the hospital, following the paramedics, the Colonel's eerie silence scary as hell. No matter how much they got up each other's butts, on that night terror and shock united them. As had their determination to act "normal" for Mom's sake during the weeks that followed—

He realized Marian was watching him, her drawn-on eyebrows pushed together behind her silver glass frames.

"I'm sure they'll give us an update soon," he said. "You want some coffee or something?"

Her gaze returning to those damn doors, Laurel's grandmother firmly shook her head.

The admitting nurse had told her she was welcome to come with Laurel into the exam room, if she wanted, but Laurel had said absolutely not. Kindly enough, but firmly. After watching the old gal do her pacing thing for the past hour, Tyler could understand why. Her worrying would've driven him insane, too.

But at least she did worry. At least Laurel *had* her, no matter how nuts the batty old woman made her.

Finally, Marian plunked her bony little butt beside him, heaving a breath that smelled of peppermint. "You don't have to stay, you know. You probably need to get back to the party."

"I'm good," he said, even though he wasn't. At all. Not only for the aforementioned reasons, but for a whole bunch more he didn't want to examine too closely. "And anyway, I brought you over, remember? In your car?"

"Oh, right. Forgot." She frowned at the doors again. "How hard can it be to tell us something? Is she in labor or not?"

Talk about being out of his depth. Although Laurel hadn't seemed to be in any real distress on the way to the hospital that he could tell. Tight-lipped, yes, but not like he imagined a woman in labor would be. Didn't they tend to moan and scream a lot? So his guess was that she'd been more pissed than anything. "Not that I know anything about this...but maybe they're not sure, either—?"

"This is all my fault," Marion huffed, and Tyler frowned. "Excuse me?"

Her bright red mouth thinned. "Oh, it would bug me to *death,* seeing her sit at home night after night, acting like she was perfectly content with her life when I knew she wasn't. Or, when she would go out with somebody, give up on the guy before even giving him a chance. She's so damn *picky,* honestly. Always has been. Not like her mother, that's for sure..."

Realizing she was probably yammering to keep herself from thinking too hard about her granddaughter—that, or she was one of those old ladies who'd share her innermost thoughts with anyone who'd stay still for more than thirty seconds—Tyler leaned forward to leaf through a two-year-old *Entertainment Weekly* on the table in front of them, figuring eventually the old girl would run out of steam. And the talking was better than the pacing.

"...and I probably would've let it go," she went on, "except, like I said, I knew she wasn't happy. Or at least, not as happy as she could be. Because when she was a little girl—before she came to live with me, I mean—she'd talk and talk and *talk* about how she couldn't wait to get married, what her wedding would be like, how many children she wanted. Five," Marian said with a chuckle. "Can you imagine? And she went out plenty when she was a teenager. Although I was a real buzzkill, I wouldn't let her date until she was sixteen. But she never had a serious boyfriend that I could tell. At first I was glad, figuring...well. You know. Then..."

Underneath a helmet of shimmering white waves, the

old woman's forehead knotted. "Then, after college, she moved to the city for a few years. By this time she was in her twenties, and I started to nag her…" Laughing softly, she laid a warm hand on Tyler's forearm. "You know, about whether she'd met any nice young men. Only she'd be so *cagey,* never really answering me. Frankly, for a while I wondered if she might be gay but didn't want to tell me."

Not at all what he'd been expecting. "What?"

"Well, the thought crossed my mind. It seems to be the thing these days, doesn't it?" she said, and Tyler hid his smile, even as he caught the chuckle from the black woman across the room from them. "Not that I would have minded, not in the least. People can't help being who they are. As long as you're a good person, what the hell do I care who you sleep with?"

Hugging that bright pink purse, she touched Tyler's wrist again. "And it's *so* much better now than it was in my time, thank God, when everybody *knew* but it was all hush-hush. So silly. And sad. Anyway," she sighed out, "I finally asked Laurel one day, point blank, if that was the case. She laughed and said no…but that's when I first saw it. The sadness in her eyes. And as her old girlfriends all started getting married, asking her to be in their weddings, I saw that sadness a lot. Not that anyone else would have probably noticed, but it broke my heart. Because it was exactly like when day after day would go by, and her father wouldn't call…."

Tyler glanced away, his own chest constricting.

"I had such a wonderful childhood," Marian said, shaking her head, "with parents who doted on me. And my marriage… Sometimes I can't believe how blessed I was, even if it didn't last as long as I would have liked. So it's sometimes hard for me to relate to what that poor girl must have felt when she realized her parents' marriage was a sham,

that her father had only stuck around out of duty, but he
didn't love her *or* her mother. And then to repeat history,
in a way, with this Barry person... Such a shame."

Tyler frowned. "I don't understand. She said it was
pretty...casual."

Marian looked at him. "Did she now?" Huffing a breath,
she turned away. "Not that I'm surprised she'd try to shield
her heart. Because believe me, honey, she was head over
heels with that man. And I don't care if I'm not supposed to
tell or not, it's the truth. Still might be, for all I know...it's a
forbidden subject these days. Between her and me, at least."

"But...she told me she knew he didn't want kids—"

"And she did. Does. Yeah. And what does it say about
her that she loved the dirtwad enough to sacrifice that for
him? A word clearly not part of dirtwad's vocabulary."
She shook her head, then sighed. "He didn't get himself
fixed on a whim, after all. Although I don't suppose anyone would."

"So...the baby really was an accident."

Marian laughed. "Oh, honey—half of all babies are 'ac-
cidents,' happy or otherwise. And my granddaughter decided to roll with the punches, God love her. The man *she
loved,* however, was having none of it." Her mouth twisted.
"And the saddest thing of all is that I set her up with the
bastard."

Tyler's brows sprang up. "Really?"

"Yep. He's the son of one of the gals in my book club.
I've known her forever...she's a doll. And Barry seemed
plenty nice the one time I met him when he came to take
his mother to lunch." She opened her purse, took out a tin
of breath mints. Popped one in her mouth, offered the tin
to Tyler. He shook his head, *no.* "I had no clue about the
vasectomy, of course—his mother and I aren't *that* close.
I knew he had two kids from his previous marriage—God

knows Norma showed me pictures often enough—but how many men have second families these days? Plenty. To prove they still got it, or something. And he was educated, smart, not bad looking...the whole package. A nice boy, she could do a lot worse, I thought. And he and Laurel certainly seemed to hit it off...."

She squeezed shut her eyes, then opened them again. "And if I hadn't *meddled,* kept my nose to myself, none of this would've happened. Not that I'm not thrilled about being a great-grandma, I don't mean that. But I certainly never meant for Laurel's heart to get broken in the process.... Oh!" she said, poking Tyler as a white-coated, middle-aged Asian gal pushed through the swinging doors. "Maybe that's us!"

"Mrs. McKinney?"

Marian was instantly on her feet. "That's me! So are we going to have a baby tonight?"

The doctor laughed. "No, thank goodness, since your granddaughter's not due for several weeks yet. I really didn't think she was in labor when she came in, but it seemed wise to monitor her, just to be sure." Smiling, she clasped the chart to her chest. "And as I suspected, she was only having upper abdominal contractions, probably brought on by the heat and being on her feet too much. And Junior's head is pressing against her spine, which is causing the backaches. Nothing really unusual, to be honest. Although I will say..."

Dark eyes swung between Tyler and Laurel's grandmother, then back again. "You might want to keep an eye on her, make sure she doesn't overdo things for the next few weeks. To keep her more comfortable, if nothing else. And don't let her try to convince you she doesn't need someone to help out—which she probably will if her time here is any indication—because she does. You want her strong and healthy and rested for when she does this for real."

"Got it," Marian said, and the doctor smiled.

"Otherwise, both mama and baby are doing great, so I think we're good to send her home." She briefly touched Marian's shoulder. "Laurel's getting dressed, she'll be out shortly."

And indeed, before the doctor disappeared down the hall to the nurses' station, Laurel came through the doors, looking more chagrined than anything else.

Tyler, however, felt like somebody'd reached inside his head and rearranged his brain. First off, he was mad that she'd essentially lied to him about her relationship with this Barry person, even though he knew that was stupid. She could tell him anything she wanted, or not, what difference did it make? It wasn't like they had a relationship or anything, she didn't owe him squat. But what made him even more mad, was that the jerk was apparently all *Whoops, sorry* about getting her pregnant, like he figured since he didn't *want* her to be pregnant, it was somehow okay for him to pretend she wasn't? That it never happened? That the kid— *his* kid—didn't exist? Then to hear her grandmother talk about how Laurel had always wanted a husband and kids—

No, maybe Tyler couldn't see himself as a family man. But that didn't mean he didn't understand how other people would want that. Or that he didn't feel like Laurel had gotten a raw deal.

Hell, in her position? He'd probably fudge the facts, too. Just like he had, come to think of it.

Laurel wearily accepted her grandmother's hug, then loudly exhaled. "Well, that was a spectacular waste of time. Nothing like being a big ol' party pooper." She looked at Tyler, and more stuff happened in his head. Like…he cared what happened to this woman, maybe. "I feel terrible—"

"Yeah, I'm sure Kelly will never forgive you," he said. "'Cause she's real self-centered like that."

She gave him a little smile then looked down at her feet, stuffed again in those stupid shoes. "I cannot walk another step in these things, they are so coming off—"

"Not on this floor, they're not," Marian said. "Do you have any idea how many germs are in hospitals?"

"But— Oh!" she said as Tyler swept her up in his arms. "Tyler! For heaven's sake, I must weigh five million pounds! I'll give you a hernia!"

"Get her shoes," he said to Marian, who immediately complied with his request, tugging first one, then the other off and stuffing them inside her purse.

"Let's blow this joint," the old gal said, and started for the exit. Tyler followed, feeling like some hero in a movie. Especially when, on another gasp, Laurel linked her hands around his neck—for security, probably, since he might've been bouncing her a little—then stared at the side of his face.

"Really?"

He hoisted her slightly as they all marched through the automatic doors, people gawking and/or grinning at them as they passed. "You got a problem," he said as they trekked toward the car, parked in the open-air lot, "take it up with management."

With a little hiccup, Laurel laid her head on his shoulder, surprising the crap out of him. "Thank you," she whispered.

"No problem."

Except it was. A helluva lot more than he'd ever let on. Because being a hero—or at least, playing one as he carted this woman across St. Luke's parking lot—was so not part of his skill set.

Chapter Six

It was almost dark before Laurel finally convinced Gran to leave, she'd be fine. Five minutes later, in her nightie and robe, she passed out in the übercomfy, ancient armchair that as a kid had been her fave place to curl up and read, next to Gran's picture window in her living room. So God knows what time her phone rang, startling her awake. As well as her sweet little parasite, who walloped her a good one in her bladder, making her need to pee. Drat.

Muttering not nice words, she checked her phone. Tyler. Who, before she could mumble hello, said, "Room service."

"Again?"

"Blame Kelly. They had a crapload of food left over—in part because three of us weren't there to eat it—"

"Really? You're pinning this on me?"

"—so she made me come over and take some. And told me to take it to you, pronto. And she was gonna check with you to make sure I did. God, she's worse than my brothers. And Boomer and I are standing on your porch, by the way."

"It's…" She blearily peered at her phone. "Late."

"So?"

Sighing, Laurel heaved herself to her feet—because she'd become one with the chair, not because she was pregnant—and trudged to the front door. The instant she opened it, many pounds of joyous dog exploded into the living room, spinning in circles before planting his wriggling butt on the floor in front of Laurel, grinning like a goon.

Laurel tried to lean forward to pet the beast, except her bladder had other ideas. On another sigh she straightened, then started for the potty. With only the briefest glance at the bulging bag in Tyler's hands.

"Good God. How much is in there?"

"Enough to last you at least until tomorrow morning."

"You are so dead," she said, continuing her trek. A couple minutes later she returned, much relieved, somewhat awake and, yes, starving. Tyler was in her kitchen, again, laying out another feast on her table. Like a panting, drooling sphinx, Boomer lay on the tile floor, totally oblivious to Laurel's entrance, so intent was he on his master's every move.

And now that Laurel was awake, she was every bit as fixed on Tyler's actions as the dog was, a shiver skittering over her skin at the memory of being in his arms, against that chest, and hunger of another kind reared its nasty little—okay, not so little—head. Yes, yes, he'd only been doing the good guy thing and all that. But still. It'd been nice, for a moment there, to feel safe, and cared about. To pretend.

"Honestly, you didn't have to do this."

"One word—Kelly. And besides, what did you have for dinner?"

"Food. And I sent my grandmother home because

I couldn't take the hovering. But at least she's family... What's that?"

He held up a largish, square container. "Wedding cake. Need I say more?"

On a defeated sigh, Laurel sank onto one of the kitchen chairs. There were many things she could resist, but cake was not one of them. Or cookies. Or pie. Chocolate silk, especially—

"So Kelly tells me she's throwing you a shower?"

He set a plate of food large enough to feed Iowa in front of her, as well as a chilled bottle of water, then sat across the table with his own.

"She would *like* to throw me a shower. I haven't decided yet whether that's a good idea."

Chomping on a chicken leg, Tyler frowned, then took a sip of his water. "Because...?"

"Because it just feels..." She picked up one of the kebabs, slid off a shrimp and popped it into her mouth. "Pushy."

"Yeah, that's Kelly, all right—"

"I didn't mean her! I meant me! I'd feel like..." She blushed. "Like a charity case."

"Then you need to get over yourself. I mean, did it occur to you how happy it would make *her,* to do this for you? For the kid?" he said, waving the chicken bone at her belly. "She also said..."

He stuffed a bite of potato salad in his mouth, then got up and walked out of the kitchen. She and the dog looked at each other, then followed suit, to find Tyler standing in front of The Room. He flicked on the overhead.

"This gonna be the nursery?"

"Yes. And one day I might even pick a color. So I can paint it."

Tyler glanced at her belly, then walked over to the half

dozen paint samples on the bare windowsill. He picked one up, a dusty blue. "The light sucks, for sure, but…" He splayed the other samples, tapping the yellow for a moment before holding out the blue. "Yeah. This one. We'll go get the paint tomorrow morning, I'll start on it soon as we get back—"

"Says who?"

"Me. And the E.R. doctor."

"She told you to paint the baby's room?"

"She told your grandmother and me you're supposed to take it easy for the next few weeks. Because you don't want those contractions to start up again, right? And Kelly said you told her you're having trouble making decisions, and I don't, so…"

He waggled the chip. "Since it was already in here, I'm gonna assume you didn't hate it. Right?"

"No, of course not, but—"

"And you're gonna let Kell give you that shower, and let people bring you food and crap, and do all the stuff for you the baby's father should be doing…."

He jerked away, his mouth set in a hard line as he put the swatch back down, and Laurel's heart knocked in her chest. "Ty? What's this all about?"

His shoulders lifted with his breath before, with a glance, he brushed past her to return to the kitchen. She found him slouched in the chair, his arms crossed over his chest, one leg jutting out underneath the table. "Your grandmother…she got to talking, while we were waiting. In the E.R."

"Oh, God," Laurel said, taking her seat again, as well. "I'm almost afraid to ask… What did she say?"

"That you were serious about whatshisname. Barry. That you still might be."

"Thanks, Gran," she muttered.

"So she was right?"

After a moment, she nodded.

"So why'd you tell me—"

"That it was casual? Oh, I don't know…maybe because I didn't want to come across as some brokenhearted sad sack? But…yeah. Corny and pathetic as it sounds, I'd given him my heart. Since, to be blunt, I wouldn't have given him anything else otherwise."

"And then he abandoned you."

The coldness underlying his words almost mitigated the pain they caused. But not the anger.

"I told you, I knew going in Barry didn't want children. And I'd accepted that. True, when I found out I was pregnant, I hoped he'd change his mind…but he didn't. And yes, that hurt. Like holy hell. So I had a choice—suck it up and move on, or infect myself, and my baby, with a bunch of negative feelings. No matter how justified," she said when Tyler opened his mouth again.

"So, what? You simply decided you didn't love him anymore?"

"What I decided was not to let my feelings lead me around by the nose. That I was stronger than they were."

"So if he was to show up tomorrow and say he'd changed his mind, would you slam the door in his face?"

How often had she asked herself exactly that? At least in the beginning, before hope gave way to logic. Even so…

"For Jonathon's sake? No. Probably not."

Tyler got up again, his hands shoved into his back pockets as he walked over to the uncovered patio door, facing the dark yard.

"He is Jonny's father," Laurel said. "And after everything you said, I'd think you of all people would be on board with that."

"Meaning you'd forgive him?"

"It's called moving on, Tyler." He looked at her over his shoulder, his expression clearly saying he wasn't buying it. Not that she blamed him. "Look, I have no trouble owning my serious error of judgment—one I hope to God I never make again—but I'm dealing with the consequences as best I can. And Barry…he has to sort through his own junk. I can't do that for him. Would I let him back into *my* life? I don't know, to be honest. I obviously thought he was a good person at the time or I wouldn't have gotten involved with him."

"And you still think he's that person?"

"Considering his current state of asshattery, you mean? I think he's scared and angry and…I don't know. But somebody has to be the grown-up here, and it looks like I'm it. And all I can do is take things one day at a time."

When he turned back to the window, his jaw clenched, Laurel pushed herself out of her seat and came close to gently lay a hand on his back, the muscles taut underneath his gray T-shirt. She knew so little about him, really, other than what she'd seen—his generosity and kindness, a protective streak a mile wide, a bone-deep goodness at complete odds with his conviction that he'd been a pain in the butt as a kid. So she could only guess that whatever was causing the obvious torment she heard in his voice, saw in his body language, about a subject that—to be honest—had nothing to do with him, stemmed from something in his past.

And she ached for him.

Dammit.

Laurel rubbed the space between those rock-hard shoulder blades, just for a moment, then lowered her hand to his, forcing their fingers to braid. As his gaze veered to hers, Boomer came up and swiped his tongue across their entwined hands, then returned to the table and sank onto the floor with a groan. Tyler's eyes followed his dog, one side of his mouth curled up. It was so obvious how much he cared about that dog. How much he cared, period, she thought as annoyance shunted through her, that she cared, too. More than she wanted to. And heaven knows more than she should, since it wasn't as if she didn't have enough garbage of her own to deal with without trying to pick through someone else's.

And yet, she gently squeezed his hand—instead of going with her first instinct, which was to smack the doofus until he screamed like a girl—and said, "This isn't really about me, is it—?"

Tyler's phone buzzed. He let go of her hand to dig it out of his pocket, his brow furrowing as he glanced at the text message.

"It's... There's a problem at the, um, warehouse, I need to go."

"Oh! Nothing serious, I hope?"

"Probably not, but..." Still frowning, he glanced at her belly for a moment. "I shouldn't be too long. Call me if you need anything, okay? Otherwise I'll be here at nine tomorrow morning, we'll go get the paint. That work for you?"

"Uh, sure, nine's good—"

"Then we're all set. Boomer! Let's go, buddy..."

And he was gone.

Half confused, half pissed, Laurel slammed leftovers back into containers, cramming them into her fridge before tromping to her deck. Her arms tightly crossed over The Bump, she stared out into her dark yard. Thoughts and feelings roared inside her head like a tornado, the inner noise almost drowning out the muffled thrum of distant highway traffic, the sporadic chirping of a nearby cricket. The gentle gurgling of the lion's head fountain.

Because she didn't get it, she really didn't. Okay, what

she didn't get, was Tyler. Why he'd appointed himself her guardian, why he cared. Especially since he'd made it perfectly plain that caring would only, ever, go so far. And since things of that nature weren't looking too good from her side, either—

Squeezing shut her eyes, Laurel hauled in an all-the-way-to-her-toes breath, then exhaled the aggravation and stress, a trick Gran had taught her years ago. Along with the Count Your Blessings game, which used to make Laurel roll her eyes until she finally realized Gran knew what she was talking about. So she mentally rattled off her current list: a job she loved, a ten-year-mortgage, a healthy baby growing inside her. A grandmother she adored, who didn't let her get away with squat. And, yes, Tyler. Who, besides having the coolest dog ever and not being bad on the eyes, brought her food. And fountains. And, fine, friendship. A little wonky though that friendship might be.

So. A lot to be grateful for. And yet…

Was it asking too much of the universe to let her have, just once, a reasonably *normal* relationship?

She lifted her gaze to the milky sky, but the universe wasn't answering.

Starla was next door to hysterical by the time Tyler arrived, wild-haired in a billowing nightgown as she stood on her porch with that ugly-ass cat of hers—who wasn't looking any too happy, either—clutched to her chest.

"I have no idea how it got in!" she cried before he even shut his car door. "I'm sitting there, watching a DVD, and suddenly this, this *thing* swooped between me and the TV and I nearly had a heart attack. Thought it was a bird until I heard that…that noise they make."

She shuddered, making the cat squirm. And growl. Tyler knew better than to try petting the damn thing, even when it wasn't stressed out. Just as well, though, Starla hadn't let him go after the bat, even if his rabies shots were up-to-date.

"Where is it now?" he asked, pulling on a pair of heavy work gloves as he approached.

"In the house. Somewhere."

Great.

"Got a coffee can? Something I can catch it in if I need to?"

"The one in the fridge is nearly empty, dump out what's left on a plate or something."

Tyler cautiously opened the front door, the small living room pulsing from the flickering wide-screen TV in the far corner. Otherwise, it was totally dark. And dead still. No swooping. He wasn't a novice at this bat-riddance thing—one had invaded the Colonel's house when he was a kid, and again in his own place a year or so ago—but it wasn't his favorite sport, either. Tricky little devils, bats were. Although at least it was good to know they were rarely rabid. The little ones, anyway. If this was one of those jumbo jet dudes, Starla would just have to move.

"Okay, I'm leaving the door open to give it a chance to find its way out." At Starla's gasp, Tyler chuckled. "It's not gonna attack you, I swear. Or get in your hair. So chill."

"Could… Can I wait in your truck?"

"Sure, it's open."

He waited until two tons of metal and glass stood between her and mayhem, then went back inside, turning on a few more lights on his way to the kitchen. Wherever the thing was, it was probably more confused than Starla was scared. And hungry, wondering where all the bugs were.

The can emptied, Tyler thoroughly checked the kitchen, closing the door behind him. Same with the two bedrooms, then the bathroom. Far as he knew, Mr. or Ms. Bat was still in the living room.

Somewhere.

But as he was pondering how one might call a bat, the thing zipped past him to land on the striped valance over the picture window. "Gotcha," Tyler muttered, grabbing a magazine off the coffee table and plopping the can over the little sucker. The magazine securely covering the opening, he carted can and bat way out to the street and removed the magazine. The thing pinged around in the can for a second, then flapped off into the Jersey night. A moment later Starla—still clutching the cat—zipped from the car and up her steps to slam shut her door.

The cat, who'd clearly had enough, *rrrwwed* and wriggled free, thudding onto the porch floor before stalking off, tail twitching, to collapse a few feet away to recover from her ordeal. Starla collapsed as well, into a wicker chair, her hand pressed to her chest.

"Thank you *so* much. If you hadn't come over…well. I'm not sure what I would've done. Slept out here, I suppose."

"Right. Because the only bat in Jersey was in your house."

She let out a soft laugh. "Good point." The cat, apparently already recovered, jumped right back in her mistress's lap. "You want something to drink?"

"No. Thank you. It's late—"

"Of course, you're right— Oh! I hope I didn't wake you—?"

"You didn't, it's okay. And you know you can call me anytime."

Starla stroked the cat for several seconds before saying again, on a heavy sigh, "Well. Thanks."

"You're welcome," Tyler said, the words all twisted up inside him, like they always were. Because he knew that second thanks had nothing to do with him getting a bat out of her house and everything with trying to figure out who they were to each other.

His duty done, he walked back to his car and climbed inside, giving her a little wave as he backed out, drove off. Except—and here was the weird thing—that's not what he'd wanted to do. What he'd wanted, was to say "sure" to that drink, then sit and talk to this slightly crazy woman about all the crazy stuff going on inside his own head… about Laurel, who seemed to have the crazy stuff figured out a helluva lot better than he did.

And he didn't know what to do about that. Her.

Hell, he didn't know what to do about anything.

He glanced in the rearview mirror to see Starla still on her porch, like maybe she was watching him—it was hard to tell from this far away, in the dark—and his chest got all tight with things he didn't know how to say, questions he still couldn't figure out how to ask. Aside from the biggie, which she still refused to answer. Except, now more than ever, being around Laurel…it made him want to fix stuff. Not sidestep it, or run from it, or pretend this thing he called a life was anything more than a bunch of BS, but figure out how to make things better. How to *be* better. The woman was a freaking inspiration, is what, the way she refused to feel sorry for herself. And he'd look at her and something like…like hope flickered to life, that maybe—

An image of her pregnant belly slammed into his brain.

Tyler shoved out a frustrated breath. Because wanting something, and thinking you have any *business* wanting it, were two entirely different things.

So tomorrow he'd pick Laurel up, and they'd go to the store, and he'd paint this baby's room, like he'd promised.

But beyond that…well. He'd learned a long, long time ago the folly of trusting *maybe*.

And this time was no different.

By the time Tyler arrived the next morning, Laurel had more or less made peace with the universe. Not that she and the cosmos didn't still have some heavy-duty issues to work out—she was still waiting for it to get back to her on the normal relationship thing—but for now she was just grateful that somebody other than her was going to paint this kid's room. And if that somebody happened to have most excellent abs and a truly fine backside, all the better. Because her motto was, if the universe gives you eye candy, snack away.

Especially if the eye candy was apparently going to pretend last night's weirdness had never happened.

"So…you're good to go?" he said. With an oddly subdued grin, Laurel thought. "No more funny business with…" He nodded toward her bump.

"Not even a twinge." She patted her tummy. "He even let me sleep last night. Only got up to pee once."

"O-kay, let's get going, then," Tyler said, adding, "Let's take my truck, the air-conditioning in yours sucks."

"You've never been in my car, how would you—? Oh. Gran."

"Yep."

Honest to Pete. At this rate he was going to know when she'd had her first period. However, since it was true, the air-conditioning in her car was pitiful, she followed him to his driveway, where he opened the passenger side door, then helped—okay, hoisted—her up and inside. Although at least he had the courtesy not to grunt. He did, however, suggest they stop for breakfast.

"Because I'm down to Cheerios, and that ain't gonna cut it if I'm going to be painting all day."

Settled into the seat, Laurel looked into those twinkly green eyes, shadowed under the brim of his ball cap, and was instantly besieged by a veritable horde of naughty thoughts. Also, hunger. Of the stomach kind.

"I am so in," she said, banishing the naughty thoughts to Outer Mongolia. "That pancake place out on the highway?"

"Done," he said, shutting her door and walking around to get in behind the wheel. She had to admit, she kinda liked being up this high. Not to mention letting somebody else drive.

"My treat, by the way," she said after they'd pulled out of the driveway.

"You don't have to—"

"Hey. You're painting my child's room. You gave me a fountain. You keep bringing me food. The least I can do is buy you breakfast."

A slight grin tugged at his beautiful, beautiful mouth. A beautiful, beautiful mouth on a beautiful, beautiful man. Not *boy*.

Hormones, take note.

"You clearly have no idea how hungry I am," he said, and Laurel shut her eyes for a moment, thinking, *Do not go there. Do not go anywhere. Do not*—

Then she opened them and said, "And I bet I can match you pancake for pancake. With an omelet and bacon on the side."

The grin widened. "So all those stories about pregnant women eating like lumberjacks are true?"

"God, yes. In fact, the first thing that tipped me off that I wasn't just 'late' was one night when I ordered a pizza, thinking I'd have leftovers for lunch the next day. Ate the whole thing at one sitting. And not some lame, one-topping thing, either. A supreme, thank you. *Large. And* an entire bag of popcorn an hour later."

"Damn."

"Yeah. It was awesome. The belches afterward, especially. I felt like a freaking frat boy." When he shook his head, she smiled at him. "What?"

"You are too much. And I mean that as a compliment. You're like...a guy."

"I'm...flattered?"

Even though he chuckled, he also blushed, which she found highly amusing. He flexed his hand around the steering wheel. "I've...never met a woman like you. Hell, anybody like you."

"Perhaps you should reconsider where you've been looking," she said, only to immediately think *What the hell?* Like she'd opened her mouth, but her grandmother's words had fallen out. "Sorry, that was out of line—"

"No, it wasn't. Well, yeah, maybe it was. Except...you're right. Not that I was fully aware of that until two seconds ago, but...yeah. Wow," he said softly, like a whole new world had opened up inside his head.

And since she was already in for a penny... "Got any idea why?"

A long pause preceded, "Maybe because I wasn't sure what to do with what I might find in the right place?"

Laurel's laugh came out all weird-sounding. "And *I'm* not sure I want to know what that means."

"S'okay. Since I'm not sure I could explain it. But, yeah. Or, no, I guess. I've never had a serious girlfriend. Never wanted one. So I had to be careful who I dated, that they weren't expecting forever, either."

She glanced over, caught the frown. Wondered if he had any idea how...flat he sounded. She hesitated, then said,

"But you've got guy friends, right? Somebody to hang out with, watch the game, whatever."

"I've got my brothers."

"Not the same thing."

"True. But…what you said, about your girlfriends all getting married? Same here. Except, well. The guys. And the few who aren't…" His shoulders bumped. "I'd rather be alone, frankly. I mean, I like to have fun, sure, but…it's like their brains shorted out ten years ago. That's the place you meant, right?" he said, nodding toward the enormous sign ahead on their right.

"Um, yeah. That's it."

Tyler pulled into a parking space; since her center of gravity was already in another solar system, Laurel waited for Tyler to help her out. But in the tight space between the two parked cars, although he offered his hand for her to grasp, she stumbled anyway, so his other hand went to her waist…and then he didn't let go right away—

"You okay?" he said, his breath in her hair as she slightly staggered, then righted herself, The Bump knocking against his stomach.

"Of course," she said, meeting his gaze. And this time, his eyes weren't twinkling. This time, she saw…more. Confusion, maybe. Lust, definitely, which almost made her laugh out loud, considering she felt about as sexy as a bag of potatoes.

Mostly, though, she saw yearning. For what, she wasn't sure. And neither was he, she imagined. But that longing… it not only touched her heart, but came awfully close to breaking it—

"Hey, lovebirds!" said some paunchy dude on the sidewalk. "If it's okay with you, I'd like to get to my car sometime today?"

"Sure, no problem," Tyler said, setting Laurel aside to

slam shut the open door, then hustling her toward the restaurant before Irked Dude ruptured something. She wasn't
sure whether to be relieved or hugely annoyed.

Once inside, however, where they had to wait in the
jammed lobby for a free table, she got over herself enough
to realize hunger—and, okay, a still-bruised heart—had
momentarily made her hallucinate, seeing and hearing
things that weren't there. The longing, yes—that, she hadn't
imagined. But not a longing for *her*. Big difference.

But you know what? Tyler had already proven himself a
good friend. Someone she could rely on. Could trust. And
right now, a *friend* is what she needed, more than anything.

And if she kept telling herself that, she might almost
believe it.

Chapter Seven

She'd had no idea, Tyler was sure, how close he'd come to kissing her, back there in the parking lot. The way the sun'd been shining in her hair, making it look so glossy and smell so damn good…the way he'd felt practically sucked into those blue eyes…

Holy crap.

So thank God that guy had come along, blasting the moment outta the water. It'd been bad enough, Tyler saying all that "a woman like you" stuff. Because what the hell, right? Especially considering that talking-to he'd given himself the night before. Seriously, it was like something had chewed up the cable between his brain and his mouth.

He pounded the lid back on the paint can, the plastic drop cloth scrunching underfoot as he carefully set the can in the corner by the closet. At least breakfast had been… uneventful. Watching Laurel pack it away, though… He smiled again, remembering. She was just so *herself,* he guessed was the best way to describe it. Like she really didn't give a rat's ass what anybody else thought about her. Or her choices.

Funny how at first he'd thought she was antisocial or something, because he'd seen her so rarely after she'd moved in. Now he realized nothing could be further from the truth. Actually, she was probably one of the most open people he'd ever met.

In fact, he thought more about their conversation in the restaurant, how they'd switched from subject to subject, never running out of things to talk about. How she had no trouble expressing her opinions, but not in that judgmental way most people did, where they assumed you thought the same way they did. Or should. Not Laurel. Oh, she'd poke around inside his head, asking him why he'd come to the conclusions he had, but then she actually listened to his answers. Like she respected him. What he thought.

What was weird, though, was how that openness made him feel both good and uneasy at the same time. Granted, after a lifetime of people keeping secrets from him, of dating girls who only let him see what they wanted him to see—he frowned at the far wall, making sure he hadn't missed any spots—in many ways it was a relief, being around somebody who wasn't into guessing games. That, he liked. A lot. But she also made him feel slightly off balance. Not intentionally or anything, and it wasn't that he minded being challenged, being forced to use his brain instead of his charm or BS or whatever. But the more they talked, the more obvious it became that there was no way in hell he'd ever catch up to her.

That he'd ever be her equal.

Like she'd known he was thinking about her, Laurel—with Boomer beside her—appeared at the doorway, wearing that I-got-this expression he'd finally decided was her default mode. Sure, she got pissed sometimes, same as anybody else. Except…she didn't stay pissed. Not that he could tell, anyway. Or go looking for things to get pissed about.

She handed him a water bottle. "Figured you could use this about now."

"Thanks," he mumbled, taking the bottle and wrenching off the cap, slugging half of it down while frowning at the damn wall like it was gonna talk to him.

Because he was conflicted about that, too. Not the wall, Laurel's calmness in the face of things no reasonable person should be calm about. Maybe he'd promised to keep his yap shut about the subject, but it still bugged him, how she'd let Jonny's father off the hook. Man, it was killing him not to go all Sopranos on her, pull a full-blown *Whatsamatterwithyou?* fit to make her see reason. To let him and Matt go after the guy's sorry ass. Because Matt and his cronies in the department could find him, Tyler was sure they could. Except even that made him feel several rungs lower on the evolutionary scale than she was—

"Tyler? Everything all right?"

He turned, noticing that Boomer had planted his butt right beside Laurel, his head slightly tilted, like he was wondering the same thing. "Yeah. Sure. What about you? You look a little flushed."

"That's called glowing. At least, that's what I'm gonna go with." She leaned farther into the room. "Oh, wow… this looks *so* good."

"So the color's okay? 'Cause sometimes, it doesn't look the way you think it's going to from the paint chip—"

"No. It's perfect. Exactly what I saw in my head." She laughed. "When I thought about *blue,* anyway."

Man, he did like that laugh. The way her eyes got all crinkly…

"When I get the trim painted, it'll look even better. Like

right out of a decorating show." He frowned at the floor, scuffed all to hell underneath the rumpled plastic. For whatever reason, the rest of the house was carpeted—a hideous Berber that'd seen better days ten years ago—but somebody'd ripped it up in here, leaving the floor naked and wounded. Which in turn hurt something deep in his soul. "If you want, I could refinish the floor—"

"Oh! No, you've already done so much—"

"It wouldn't take that long. It's a small room. And the wood's good." He squatted to lift the plastic. "Maple, looks like. Definitely worth refinishing. I did the floors in my house, and they came out great. In fact, at some point you should consider doing the rest of them, too. It'd definitely add value to the house."

"In other words, the carpet's from hunger."

"That, too."

"I'll...think about it," she said. "In the meantime, come eat lunch. Outside, it's nice under the tree. Sandwiches and chips, nothing fancy. And don't even think about declining. At this rate I'll owe you meals until we're both eligible to move into Gran's place."

The dog preceding them, Tyler helped Laurel cart their food out and down to the yard, where they set everything on the picnic table. And she was right...it was nice out here—the leaves quivering in the breeze, the fountain gurgling away. Like a pretty little park. Except...

"All that rain we've been getting, your lawn needs to be mowed again—"

"Good thing I already hired Dawson next door to do it tomorrow, huh?"

"Dawson? You're not serious?"

"What's wrong with Dawson?"

"Other than he's trouble waiting for a place to happen? Not a thing."

"And why do you think that?"

"Because he reminds me of me when I was that age. In fact, he's—"

"Already been in some trouble. I know. His mother told me. And how do *you* know?"

"Matt. He filled in for one of the juvie officers for a week, and Dawson was brought in for—"

"Shoplifting." At Tyler's frown, Laurel pointed to her face. "For some reason this inspires people to tell me their deepest secrets." She lowered her hand to pick up a couple of carrot sticks, giving one to the dog. Who actually ate it. Weirdo. "Although I get the feeling Yolanda doesn't need much inspiration."

"And you still hired him?"

Her mouth twitched. "Trust me, there's nothing in my yard he can filch. Or would want to. And I doubt he'll be armed. Although if it makes you feel better I'll frisk him when he gets here—"

"He's got an attitude."

"For heaven's sake—name me a thirteen-year-old who doesn't." Her gaze narrowed. "Especially a thirteen-year-old whose father's been sick for the past two years. And if he reminds you of you, why aren't you more sympathetic?"

"You wouldn't understand."

"Not if you don't explain it, I won't."

He felt his foot pop up and down underneath the table. "Look, it's great you want to help the kid out. Really. And I am sympathetic, I'm sure he feels like life has totally screwed him over. But my loyalty's with you, not him. And I don't want you getting in over your head."

"You think I'm naive?"

And there it was. Tyler let his gaze lock with Laurel's. She looked more amused than pissed. He wasn't sure how he felt about that. "I think you're too..." He thought. "Trusting."

Breaking eye contact, she gave the last bite of her sandwich to the dog. "There's no such thing, Tyler."

"Then you are naive."

"No, I'm not." She looked up, her eyes sparkling. "Especially since you were about to say *forgiving,* weren't you? Yeah, you were...I can see it in your face."

"Fine. Whatever."

She actually laughed for a moment, then let her gaze drift to the fountain. "I used to think, when I was a kid, and I saw how my father treated my mother—by being distant, making it clear how much he resented being there—that there was something wrong with her, too, just...*taking* it like that. As I got older, though..."

A whole chip disappeared into her mouth. "For one thing," she said, chewing, "I realized she was desperately trying to keep the peace as much as she could. For my sake. But I also eventually caught on, that by her not feeding my father's fire, it usually fizzled out. Or frustrated him no end, that he couldn't get a rise out of her. Which actually gave her the upper hand, didn't it? Not only was she not afraid of him, she refused to kowtow to his bullying."

"But...if your mother was so strong, why did she stay with him?"

"I asked myself that a lot. Still do, now and then. As a kid, I never found the courage to ask her, and then she was gone, and..." She shrugged. "Maybe because she would have seen leaving as a failure? That she'd given up? Who knows? But I honestly believe she stayed because she was tough. Or stubborn," she said with a fleeting smile. "Not because she was weak. Or didn't believe she had any other options. Gran would have taken us in, in an instant. So Mom wasn't trapped, by any means."

"And—I'm sorry…but what does that have to do with Dawson?"

Her eyes met his. "I'm not blind, Ty. I'm aware of the kid's issues, that I need to be wise. But that's not the same as being afraid. Which would give him—or rather, his issues—power over me. And worse, it gives them power over *him*. I also believe—and I know this sounds nuts to a lot of people—how we see others can have a real influence how they see themselves. For good or bad."

Tyler crossed his arms. "Didn't work with your father, though, did it?"

"That wasn't the point," Laurel said gently. "The point was, it worked for my *mother*. Gave *her* dominion over the situation. And even if it didn't 'take' with my father, that doesn't mean it never does." Her shoulders bumped. "I prefer to see the good in people than the bad. And if that makes me a Pollyanna, so be it."

By now Tyler felt like the Battle of the Titans was going on beneath his skull. "I don't get it—you said yourself, you're all about being practical. How is shoving your head in the sand about people being practical? Let alone logical?"

An enigmatic smile danced across her mouth. "Because it's not about refusing to see the truth. It's about looking beneath the surface for a truth maybe others have a hard time seeing. Now," she said, clumsily extricating herself from the attached bench, "I am seriously jonesing for a Fudgsicle. Want one?"

Tyler nodded, then watched Laurel walk back to the house, unable to decide if the woman was a damned saint or completely off her rocker.

Boomer suddenly snapped ineffectually at a rogue fly buzzing round his face, before hauling himself upright to lay his slobbery chin in Tyler's lap. Sighing, Ty looked into those adoring yellow eyes and thought, *This, I can handle*. Then his gaze lifted, landing on Laurel through the kitchen window, doing some weird dance as she dug their treats out of her freezer.

Sainted, insane women, however…not so much.

By the last week of August, Laurel was seriously considering moving. As in, to anyplace where it was winter. Chile, maybe. Way up in the Andes where they wore those funny hats. Not that she'd ever been a big fan of feeling like a freshly stewed prune, but prior to this summer she'd sweat and swear and live off salads and iced tea, and she survived. Now, however, as she approached her last month of pregnancy, all she wanted to do when she heard the weatherman's gleeful prediction of "Highs in the nineties at least for the next week," was smack that cheery smile right off his face.

What Kelly had said about aliens taking over her body? So true.

Speaking of whom… "So. Will you teach me how to cook?"

Behind the wheel of her vintage minivan as they returned from Babies "R" Us, Kelly laughed. "Seriously? Everybody can cook, honey."

"In theory, maybe." Laurel shoved a hand under her damp hair, lifting it off her neck. Too long to be cool, too short to pin up. Sucked. Especially since there was clearly some sort of hormonal force field in place making her impervious to the car's air-conditioning. "In practice, not so much."

"Oh, please. If caveman—or woman—figured out that fire not only kept them from freezing to death, but also made things tasty, I think you're good. Plus, *you* can read. Which puts you at a distinct advantage over your average prehistoric goober without internet access." At Laurel's sigh, Kelly chuckled. "It will be my pleasure to teach you how to cook. But what's the occasion?"

"Impending motherhood. Kid can't live off pizza."

"Unless the pizza's homemade and loaded with the good stuff. Cheese, veggies, chicken…"

"No pepperoni? No *sausage?*"

"Nitrates, baby. Not to mention enough sodium to replenish the Dead Sea. So we do chicken. Free range, if possible."

"You have got to be kidding me."

"You sound like Matt," Kelly said, pulling into Laurel's driveway. "First time I made pizza for him, he automatically turned his slice sideways, waiting for the grease to drip off. When it didn't, he looked at me like I was trying to poison him. So I think that's where we'll start," she said, cutting the engine and pushing open her door, letting in a dragon's breath gush of hot Jersey air. Laurel made a face and Kelly laughed again. "You'll love it, I promise."

Once in the house, Kelly booked it to the bathroom while Laurel punched on the air-conditioning, then turned on the hassock fan squatting in the middle of the living room floor until the house cooled off. Grunting, she lowering herself into the armchair, as gracefully as a rhino. Not to mention as classy, spreading her knees to let the breeze swirl underneath her dress.

All her grandmother's hard work to civilize her, undone in an instant.

She heard the whoosh of the toilet, half saw Kelly zip into her kitchen. "Tea okay?" the redhead called out.

"Help yourself, but I'm good with ice water, thanks."

"You got it."

Laurel heard ice cubes clatter into the glass; a minute later, Kelly returned and handed over her drink, then flopped on the sofa to kick off her espadrilles and hike her own skirt over her knees.

"Sorry, it takes a while for the air-conditioning to kick in."

"Our house is the same way, so no worries." Twisting her own thick hair off her neck, her new friend leaned back, grinning at Laurel as she raised her glass of tea. "To surviving Babies "R" Us."

Lifting her own glass, Laurel pushed out a tired laugh. "Not to mention the traffic to get there. Was *everybody* in Jersey out today?"

"Pretty much, yeah. This is going to be so much *fun,*" she said, and Laurel sighed, thinking of the slew of regrets in response to the shower invitations Kelly had sent out the week before.

"And I told you, at the rate we're going it's going to be you, me and my grandmother. It really is a lot to expect people to schlep out here from the city. And everyone else…well. There's school, and sports, and…you know. Life."

Kelly gave her a hard look. "There will be a party, sweetie. Even if it is only us. We will play stupid games and eat until our eyes pop and, if push comes to shove, watch every movie Channing Tatum's ever been in, and it will be glorious. Anyway…now that I've seen the baby's room again, I think the light wood furniture you picked out is going to look terrific against that blue. Great color. And the rug with the dinosaurs? Adorable."

Not looking at Kelly, Laurel sipped her ice water, waiting out yet another variation of the same weird feeling she'd been having since the day the room was painted. "That's Tyler's doing."

"Yeah, he told us he'd painted the room—"

"No, he chose the color, too. Well, made the final selection. And thank God, or the room would probably still be mauve. But then—get this—he 'just happened' to be in IKEA and found that rug."

"Really."

"Yeah."

"Huh." Frowning at the coffee table, Kelly tilted her tea to her lips, then canted her gaze to Laurel. "Is there something we should know? Aside from Ty's being a closet interior designer, I mean."

Laurel laughed. She'd deliberately not brought Tyler into their nonstop conversation during the past three hours, partly because she knew it would be hard enough to focus on choosing stuff for the registry as it was, partly because, well…she wasn't sure what to say. Because frankly, she had no idea what the heck their relationship was. For sure this was nothing like any friendship she'd ever had before—although, *duh,* she'd never been friends with a *guy* before—so basically she was drifting in totally uncharted waters. With no landmarks in sight. Which, alas, was making her more bonkers than she already was.

"Other than he's kind of appointed himself my…keeper? No. Although God knows why. And you can stop rolling your eyes—"

"Sorry, automatic BS sensor."

"Then you need to have that sensor checked. Because, for one thing—" she waved her hand over her bulging middle " hello? And for another, hello, again? Older woman? Which I'm guessing he's not into."

"Five years doesn't exactly make you a cradle robber."

"Five? He's… Wait." Laurel frowned. "Thirty?"

"Hey, you can still do math. Impressive."

Laurel plucked an ice cube from her drink and threw it at Kelly, making her shriek. "So," the redhead said, fishing the melting missile from her cleavage and walking it back to the kitchen, where it pinged into the stainless sink, "now that you've crunched the numbers..." She returned, clearly unrepentant. "Are you *still* sure there's nothing going on?"

"Yep. Just like I'm *still* sure I'm pregnant."

"That, however, won't last forever."

"Promise?"

"I do." Kelly sat back down. "Of course, then you'll have leaky boobs for weeks, which can definitely put a damper on...things."

"And I still have three ice cubes left here." At Kelly's snort, Laurel propped her elbow on the arm of the chair, leaning her head in her hand. "This is a pointless conversation, you realize. I've barely even seen him in the last month."

"Because he got, what? Three out-of-town salvage bids?"

"Four," Laurel said, smiling a little, remembering Ty's whoop of delight when he'd come over to see how she was doing—while Dawson was mowing her lawn, hmm—and one of the calls had come through, that he'd gotten the bid. The way he'd grinned...and hugged her... "Even so—"

Kelly snorted into her drink, and Laurel sighed.

"Fine. I'm not going to pretend I'm not attracted, since one—"

"Nobody would believe you?"

"It's so sad. I can't walk six feet without getting winded, but my libido is supercharged."

"And Ty's not exactly ugly."

"That, too. But I think it's safe to say neither of us is what the other is looking for."

"Which would be?"

"For me? Somebody who actually wants the white picket fence experience."

"And you're sure he doesn't?"

And there was the fifty-thousand-dollar question, wasn't it? "Okay, to be honest? Way, *way* down deep? Like, to the core of the earth deep? I think he does. But I have neither the time nor energy nor inclination to go tunneling past all those layers only to get burned. Again."

She took a sip of her water, avoiding Kelly's sympathetic gaze. Girlfriend knew enough of the Barry Saga to read between the lines.

"And yet—" Kelly stretched her bare feet out on Laurel's coffee table "—he keeps hanging out. Doing stuff for you. Why do you think that is?"

"We're friends?" The other woman rolled her eyes. Laurel was tempted to lob another ice cube at her. "And if you eliminate that option, what's left?"

Kelly's brow furrowed. "I got nothing." Then her eyes veered to Laurel. "He ever talk about his history?"

"Only vaguely. Not that I haven't tried to get him to open up, but he always changes the subject." She sighed. "Food, fountains, his time…those, he shares. His thoughts? As if. Although he did make some comment, weeks ago, about having been a 'pain' as a kid." She frowned. "So I sometimes wonder if… Oh, this sounds crazy."

"Which means you now have to tell me."

Laurel smiled, then said, "Sometimes I get the feeling…it's almost like he's trying to atone for something. To, I don't know…make up for the past? Except he's certainly not a bad kid now." Kelly's brows lifted. "Okay, so not a *kid* now."

That got a soft laugh. "It's okay. It took me a minute to remember how old he was, too, when I first got back last year. Like he stalled out at twenty-five—"

"*Thank* you. The hair, for one thing."

"And the general goofiness," Kelly said, and Laurel lifted her condensation-dotted glass in agreement. "It drives Matt nuts. But…" Her face scrunched, her friend pulled her legs up under her and leaned forward. "Not sure if this will help or not, but from what I know, I don't think Tyler ever really got to *be* a kid. Not when he was one, I mean."

"Meaning?"

"You…know he's adopted, right?"

"That much he told me. When he was ten, I think he said."

"Do you know why?" When Laurel shook her head, Kelly said, "I'm not privy to the whole story, of course, but I do know he landed at the Nobles as a foster the year before, because his mother was doing drugs. And I only know *that* because Sabrina was a champion eavesdropper and we basically lived in each other's pockets. But there was also something about a cop finding him roaming the streets really late one night? And his mother had no idea he was even out?"

"Oh, my God—that's awful."

"Yeah. So CPS removed him. I actually remember when he first arrived. He was like…this scrawny, snarling stray dog who didn't trust anybody, even though he was starving. You know?"

Maybe he wasn't snarling anymore, but, yeah, Laurel thought, her eyes stinging. She knew. She'd *seen*.

"Yeah. Gran adopted a stray like that once. Wanted the food, but didn't trust us. He'd cower in a corner of the porch, growling. While wagging his tail."

"Exactly. And it seemed as if the more the Colonel and Jeanne—Jeanne, especially—would try to make him feel part of the family," Kelly said, "the more he'd say he wanted to go back. To go *home*. Those first few weeks, especially. He even ran away a couple of times, as I recall.

And Jeanne and the Colonel would haul his butt back and start over again."

Laurel cupped her belly, her heart breaking for that little boy she'd never known. Except, in a way, she did, didn't she? "And his mother…?"

"Relinquished her rights a year later. And the Nobles adopted him. Which of course was the best thing that could have happened to him."

"But…" Laurel sighed as the picture came a little more into focus. "But try explaining that to a ten-year-old boy whose mother gave him up."

"Exactly." Kelly leaned back again, the breeze from the fan stirring the ends of her hair. "And he was still a handful when I moved away two years later. And continued to be, I gather. Got into trouble at school quite a bit. Nothing horrible, just stupid pranks, ditching class— a lot—stuff like that. Mostly rebelling against the discipline he'd never had before. Meaning, against the Colonel. They butted heads constantly, until Ty moved out the instant he turned eighteen." She smiled. "His saving grace, however, was Abby, who was a toddler when Tyler arrived. For some reason she glommed on to him, and he was as patient and sweet with her as could be. It was the craziest thing, how he bonded with that baby."

"Have you seen him with his dog? Not that crazy."

"True. And they're still close. Hence their going into business together." Kelly chuckled. "Ty and Abby. Not Ty and Boomer."

"I don't know, Boomer seems to take his position as door dog pretty seriously," Laurel said, then asked, "What happened with Ty's mother, do you know?"

"Here's the interesting thing. Once she gave up her rights, Tyler stopped talking about her altogether. Or if he did, Matt and Bree never heard him. In fact, Matt said

Ty refused to see her, even after she'd been straight for a couple of years and wanted to see *him*. Which the Colonel and Jeanne totally encouraged. But a couple of years ago, apparently—before I moved back to Maple River—he decided to reconnect."

"Really?"

Kelly nodded. "I don't think they see each other too often, but she doesn't live far. In fact, I gather Ty does yard work for her, things like that…"

Laurel's heart knocked. "Is her name Starla?"

"I have no idea. Although I'm sure I could find out easily enough. What—?"

"Before he built the wall between our yards, Ty took me over to some woman's house to look at one he'd done for her. I didn't think anything of it at the time—why would I?—but now… Yeah, there was definitely a resemblance. And the way she looked at him…"

Shaking her head, Laurel set the water glass down on the straw mat covering the end table. "She seemed—no, she *was*—so…bighearted. Like her only mission in life was to make people feel better. I can't imagine…" She shook her head, then frowned. "What about his father?"

"I don't think he was ever in the picture."

"Ah. That explains a lot."

"Meaning?"

"More than once after Ty realized I was pregnant— and doing this on my own—he got on my case about trying to contact Jonny's father. Almost as though it bothers him more than it does me. Not that it *doesn't* bother me. Of course it does—this wasn't exactly how I'd envisioned doing this—but what struck me was how…*personally* he seemed to be taking it."

"And he never told you why?"

"No. Even though he had to know I would've found out

eventually. Especially considering he was the one all hot to introduce me to the family. To you all, I mean. So did he really think he could keep this a secret?"

Her toes curled around the edge of the coffee table, Kelly poked at the dot of ice in what was left in her drink before saying, "Okay…assuming, for the sake of argument, this Starla really is his birth mother—because we don't know for sure, right?" Laurel grunted. "Then…maybe Ty's not trying to keep a secret as much as he simply doesn't want to talk about it. Men are like that. Believe me, I know. They're all about doing, but chatting? God forbid. Also, maybe he didn't exactly feel comfortable introducing Starla as his birth mother to some chick he hardly knew?"

Laurel's mouth twisted. "Or maybe I'm jumping to conclusions."

"Or that." Kelly paused, then said, "So you gonna ask him?"

After a moment, Laurel shook her head. "I don't think so. Whatever his reasons for not telling me…they're his reasons. I can't very well expect him to respect my choices if I don't extend him the same courtesy. Besides, really— what business is it of mine, or anybody's, who his birth mother is? Right?"

"True," Kelly sighed out, sagging back onto the couch. The air-conditioning had done its thing, the cool air purring through the vents having a dangerously soporific effect on a pair of women already suffering from post-Babies-"R"- Us syndrome. In fact, Kelly released a huge yawn before her gaze languidly drifted to Laurel's as she took another swig of her tea. "But aren't you even a tiny bit curious now? To find out the whole story?"

"Like you wouldn't believe," Laurel said, and Kelly laughed.

But it was true—she felt as though she'd been given a

book with half the pages missing…and she'd read enough to get sucked in, whether she wanted to be or not.

When Kelly got up to go potty again, Laurel hauled her broader-than-it-used-to-be butt into the kitchen to refill her water glass. And as she stood at the sink, her gaze drifted out the patio door and toward the wall, glowing in the late-afternoon sun, where a dove was blissfully splashing about in the lion's head fountain…and she thought, *What do you want from me, Tyler Noble?*

Or, more to the point, what did she want from him—?

"So whatever happened to your grandmother's rescue pooch?" Kelly asked, joining Laurel in the kitchen. "Did he ever let anyone touch him?"

Laurel smiled. "Eventually, yeah. But it wasn't easy. Took a lot of patience." She paused. "Waiting for him to come to us."

"Bet it was worth the wait, though, huh?" Kelly asked softly, and Laurel's gaze shot to hers, then skittered away again, back to the fountain, where she could practically see Tyler, after it was installed and working, turning to her with a big thumbs-up and an even bigger grin….

"He turned out to be the sweetest, most loyal dog, ever."

"The ones you have to work the hardest to win over usually are," Kelly said, not looking at Laurel as she yanked open Laurel's fridge. "This is really pathetic."

"And your point would be…?"

The door slammed shut. A dozen take-out menus fluttered. "And you seriously have way too many of these."

"What can I say? I like variety—"

"Get your purse—we're going to the grocery store," Kelly said, traipsing to the living room to grab her own off the sofa. "The kids are with their grandmother, Matt's working late… Your first cooking lesson is about to begin.

There will probably be leftovers." She grinned. "Which you can share with Tyler."

Ah. "How's about you teach *Tyler* to cook instead?"

"Because, sweetie, that would defeat my purpose."

And she thought her grandmother was bad.

Chapter Eight

Tyler had no sooner tossed his keys onto his entryway table and turned on the air-conditioning when his doorbell rang, setting Boomer off as if a horde of Vikings were outside. Sternly commanding the dog to sit, he opened the door to see Laurel awkwardly balancing a cake carrier on top of a covered casserole dish, from which emanated the Best. Smells. Ever.

"Dinner?" she said, about the same time he also noticed Kelly's van pull out of her driveway, his sister-in-law waving as she drove off.

Ignoring the now-whimpering dog, Tyler's gaze returned to the tower of food and the woman holding it, and he felt an increasingly familiar, and annoying, wallop in his gut. They hadn't hung out much in the past month, mainly because he'd been busier than a squirrel in October, although he'd kept tabs on her the best he could. You know, as a friend. Except more and more, *friendly* wasn't exactly how he'd describe his feelings toward her. But not like he wanted to jump her bones, either— even if he was guessing her being pregnant probably had a lot to do with that. It was just...

Like...when he looked at her, all he knew was, he *wanted*. Only, he didn't know what. And right now, looking into those big blue eyes, seeing that grin, he felt a lot like his frustrated dog.

He crossed his arms and aimed for a smile. "Depends on who cooked whatever that is."

"Chicken enchilada casserole and sponge cake with lemon icing. And I did."

"All of it?"

"Yes, *all* of it. Under Kelly's eagle-eyed supervision, of course. So odds are you won't get food poisoning."

"Reassuring," he said, stepping aside to let her in. It wasn't her first time in his house—she'd come over a couple weeks ago to see the floors, although he hadn't had time to redo hers yet. And he'd told himself her amused expression as she gave the living room a once-over hadn't bothered him in the least. That it didn't matter, what she thought, it wasn't like she'd ever spend much time here.

Except after she left, he took a good, long look at the place and wondered how she hadn't laughed out loud. Or run shrieking back to her place. Which is when it occurred to him that maybe it was time to trade up from Clueless Castoff to something that looked like an adult human lived there. So he'd gone out and bought a new sofa with all the guts still intact, a couple of chairs, a rug that didn't look like it'd seen one too many frat parties. Changed out the cinder block/old-door contraption for a real coffee table. Bought some lamps, even, so he didn't have to use the overhead. Which, when on, made the room look like a pee-filled fish tank.

And if her startled look made his chest tickle, so much the better.

"Look at *this*," she said as he took the dish from her. "How'd I miss the *House Crashers* dudes?"

"Very funny," he said, and she chuckled, and it made him feel good, so he decided to go with that. He carted the cake and the casserole dish to the kitchen, setting the cake aside to remove the top from the dish…and his mouth watered from the savory scents of green chile and onion, the bubbling cheese, chunks of chicken peeking out from the curled edges of corn tortillas.

"This looks amazing. You sure you want to share it?"

Laurel waddled—yes, by now she was definitely duck-walking—into the kitchen, before, with a slight grimace, bracing against the edge of the table to lower herself to the chair. "Seriously, I cannot believe I have six weeks left. At this rate I'm gonna get stuck in doorways. And not only am I sharing, it's basically yours. Since, thanks to His Highness, I'm full after two bites these days. And Gran doesn't do onions. Or chile."

"Her loss."

"That's what I thought. The plan had been to do pizza. Except the Mexican stuff was in the same aisle as the pizza stuff, and I had a roommate from New Mexico one year who turned me on to green chile, and—" she shrugged "—we got derailed."

Tyler cut squares of the casserole and served it up, then poured them two glasses of milk. The dog sucked in a quart of slobber, looking hopeful. "Forget it, mutt. No way are you getting onions and chile. Unless you want to spend the night outside. In the next county."

Boomer seemed to consider that for a moment, then slogged to the patio door, where he lay down with a huge, pity-me groan.

Well aware that Laurel was watching him, Tyler forked in a big bite of the casserole. Chewed for a moment, then speared her with a glance.

"You really made this?"

"I really did. Even shredded the cheese. The chile's canned, of course, not fresh, but one works with what one has. Well?"

"Trust me, it will not go to waste. No, I mean it—it's freaking awesome."

Laurel grinned and took a bite of her own, nodding in agreement. "It's not bad, huh? Of course, all I did was follow Kelly's orders. God knows what it'd come to if I'd been left to my own devices." Then she pricked her fork into a blob of melted cheese before saying, "I love Kelly, I really do, and I'm so grateful you introduced us, but…man, she is one bossy chick. And why are you laughing?"

"Because when I think of her from before? When we were all kids, I mean? She was this mousy little thing, totally overshadowed by Sabrina. Who's probably always been bossy. At least, she has ever since I've known her."

"You mean," Laurel said, her eyes lowered to her plate as she cut off her next bite, "when you came to live with the Nobles?"

"Yeah," Tyler said, his own gaze dipping, as well. God knows he thought about his childhood plenty, but he'd never liked talking about it. Maybe because he didn't want to get asked questions he didn't have any real clear answers for.

And if Laurel started poking around inside his head now, it was his own fault, for introducing them to begin with.

When he dared to glance up, he saw Laurel looking at him in that steady way she had, and it *killed* him, wondering what Kelly'd told her. If anything. But he didn't dare ask, did he? Not without getting into a conversation he didn't want to have. With her or anybody.

Then, her mouth curving slightly, she scraped what was left of the cheese and sauce from her plate, sucked it off her fork. "Look," she said quietly, "if there's stuff you don't feel comfortable talking about, that's okay. But if you ever need a sounding board…I'm here."

Which is when he realized…she knew. Enough, anyway. But before he could come up with something, anything, that didn't sound totally lame, she said, on a changing-the-subject exhale, "Anyway. Kelly being bossy. She's absolutely determined to give me this shower, even though hardly anybody I've invited is coming—"

"You're kidding?"

"No, it's okay, I'm not surprised." He could tell she was disappointed, though. And that, in turn, made him want to punch something. "But whenever I even think about trying to talk Kelly out of it…I can't. Isn't that nuts?"

Partly because his tongue was burning from the chili, partly because he needed a break from those damn eyes for a second, Tyler got up to refill his milk glass. The dog scrambled to his feet, ears perked. "Trying to talk Kell out of anything's a waste of energy, believe me. But if it makes her happy…" He let the fridge door slam shut, then leaned against it to take a big swallow. "What's the big deal?"

"I know, you're right. Still, I feel bad, her going to all this trouble for basically three people." He gave her a look, and she sighed. "Fine, I'm over it. Myself, whatever. Satisfied?"

Then she leaned back, her arms crossed over The Bump, looking ironically deflated, and Tyler wanted to wrap her up in *his* arms so bad his teeth ached. Which he supposed as a friend he could do, no problem. Except even the strongest people—which God knows, Laurel was—had their weak moments. And he'd never forgive himself if he caught her in one of those and misunderstandings ensued.

So instead he held out his hand for her plate. "You want more?"

"As if," she said, then smiled, and poof! the cloud dispersed. "Although I'll make room for cake if I have to jump up and down to move the kid out of the way."

After dinner, she asked Tyler if he had any foil to wrap up a piece of cake to take to her grandmother, he could keep the rest. Tempting as that was, however—the cake was even better than the casserole—he cut a piece for himself and gave her back the carrier with the remainder. She looked at it and sighed.

"You would not believe the kitchen crap Kelly made me buy. Now I'll be guilted into figuring out what to do with it so I won't feel like I wasted my money."

He walked her outside, watching as she waddled across the grass, got into her car. Shut the door. Turned the key in the ignition.

RrrrRrrrRrrr. RrrrRrrrRrrr...

Three times, she tried. Three times, the engine said, *Nope.*

Tyler walked over, motioned for her to roll down her window. Her expression was priceless. "Need a lift?"

"You don't have to—"

"You planning on walking, what?"

She huffed a very annoyed sigh. Which was probably aimed more at the car than him, but assumptions were dangerous things. "What are you, my fairy godneighbor?"

Chuckling, he grabbed his keys and the dog's leash from the entry table, locked his door, and he and Boomer headed toward his truck. Quivering with joy, the dog jumped in; Tyler went around to the passenger side in time to see Laurel haul herself out of her car, the cake carrier a swinging blur in her hand before she steadied herself, then wobble-walked back across the grass.

"No, I'm good," she said when he tried to help her—and would someone explain to him why the more pissed a woman was, the more stubborn she got?—although she did hand him the cake. Took her a while to figure out where to put what, like a mountain climber attempting to scale a sheer cliff. But after a few seconds of under-her-breath swearing, she grabbed hold of the handlebar by the door, planted one foot on the dash and heaved herself, grunting, into her seat.

"Pleased with yourself?" he asked, handing her back the cake.

"Inordinately."

A few minutes into the drive, however, he noticed how hard she was looking out her window, and his chest cramped. "Hey—"

"No, I'm good," she said, tossing him a little smile that royally ticked him off.

"You don't have to pretend with me, Laurel. This can't be easy for you—"

"And, as everyone keeps reminding me," she said steadily, "I won't be pregnant forever."

"Not talking about that. And you know it."

Silence. He glanced over, saw her lips smashed flat. And a tear slip down her cheek.

"Aw, honey—"

"Damn you," she whispered. "I'm trying *so* hard to stay positive about this…" She shook her head, her lower lip quivering. "Then reality creeps in, that I don't know a blessed thing about taking care of babies. I never even babysat, for God's sake. And now I'm expected to keep one *alive?* To know the difference between the hungry cry and the frustrated cry and the sleepy c-cry? And the scariest thing is," she said, swiping at her eyes, "I *can't* go under, can I? Because who else does this little guy have, besides me? Gran, sure, but come on, the woman's in her eighties…" She pushed out a shaky breath, then said, "The closer I get to actually having this kid? The more I wonder what am I *thinking,* trying to go solo with this."

Her words, her tears, punched him right in the gut. And brought to mind the fear, the helplessness, in someone else's eyes, so many years ago. "You regretting your decision?" he quietly asked.

A harsh laugh preceded her troweling through her purse for a tissue. She blew her nose, then said softly, "Oh, God, Tyler—you have no idea how much I already love this little g-guy. How I can't *wait* to meet him. To hold him. And deep down I know I'll muddle through this somehow. Like a gazillion mothers before me have done. But sometimes…" Her lip started quivering again. "I wake up in the middle of the night so p-panicked I can hardly breathe."

A second or two passed, before he said, his fingers strangling the wheel, "Then it's a good thing I do know something about babies. Weird as that might sound."

She sniffed. "From your b-brother's kids?"

"Yeah. And Abby, too. She was this tiny thing when I came to live with the Nobles. Followed me everywhere, like a damn baby bird. It was either learn to change her diaper or get asphyxiated," he said, and Laurel burped out a little laugh. "So you've got me, when I'm around. And your grandmother. Who can at least handle some of the other stuff while you take care of the kid, right? And I'm sure Kelly'll be more than happy to help out, too, when she can."

"I wouldn't ask—"

"This is Kelly we're talking about. You asking isn't even part of the equation." He paused. "Same goes for me. Because this family…that's how we roll."

She blew her nose again. "Except I'm not family."

"Don't kid yourself. The minute you came to that wedding, you were family. Hell, the minute anyone walks in that *house,* they're family..."

His own words smacking him upside his head, Tyler glanced over, saw her swallow. And blink. Ignoring the stinging at the back of his own throat, he focused again on the road. "You won't be alone, honey. I promise."

After a moment, she nodded. But she didn't say another word the rest of the way there.

It was nearly dark by the time they arrived. Recognizing Laurel, the guard at the gate to her grandmother's complex waved them through. Laurel directed him to park over by the lushly landscaped, brick-fronted clubhouse, flanked by tennis courts on one side, a pool on the other, where they found the old gal enjoying the hell out of herself—along with two dozen of her compadres—at a luau-themed cookout, tiki torches, leis and all.

They were instantly swarmed, although the women weren't sure who to fawn over first—Tyler, Boomer or the Very Pregnant One, who'd apparently already won their hearts some time ago. Eventually, though, the VPO won out among the women, while Boomer found himself eating up the attention of a half dozen old men, all of whom clearly missed having their own dogs—the place allowed cats, and "those little yappy things," said one dude with a shudder that made Tyler smile—but nothing that "crapped like an elephant," as another old guy said. Boomer didn't take offense. He was mellow like that.

In any case, the place gave off good vibes, not only because the grounds really were first-rate, but because the residents were, too. He could tell. And as he watched Laurel divvy up little pieces of the cake to her fan club, heard her laughter and watched her glowing face as she accepted their praise, he noticed not only the genuine affection she and the golden girls shared, but how much they all *loved a party*....

Huh.

Smiling, he pulled out his phone and called Kelly.

The morning of the shower dawned hot and muggy, as though September hadn't yet gotten the memo that summer was supposed to be winding down by now. By this point, Laurel—who'd passed "miserable" a week ago, and she had three weeks left, God help her—was ready to go lie in a wading pool somewhere and let cabana boys bring her food and drinks until the baby slipped out. But, alas, since pools and cabana boys weren't an option, she showered, pulled on the only dress she could still fit into and wriggled puffy feet into a pair of sparkly flip-flops.

She so did not want to do this, in so many ways. But she could only imagine the trouble Kelly'd gone through, and she knew Gran would be disappointed as well if Laurel bailed. And since Kelly'd said a whole bunch of people had sent gifts, anyway, and opening them alone would be beyond depressing, she supposed she could buck up for a couple of hours.

After that, though, she was coming back home and not moving, except to go potty and forage for food, until this kid was *out.*

Since Gran had "done something" to her right foot, Laurel had agreed to pick her up in her once-more-running car—the mechanics of which Tyler had explained to her but had flown right over her head. She drove the things, other people fixed them. But not everyone could write a book, so there.

Gran was all glammed up in a new pair of beige slacks and a bright purple, much-bedazzled top, her glasses glint-

ing in the September sun as she walked out to the car. Without, it seemed to Laurel, much of a limp.

"Your foot better?"

"What? Oh. Yeah. Except when I push down on it. You
know, like when I have to use the gas pedal." They got in,
but Gran had no sooner snapped her seat belt when she
smacked her own forehead and said. "I am such a dumbbutt, I forgot I need maintenance to come look at my dishwasher. You mind stopping at the office on our way out?
It'll only take a minute."

"No problem. You mind if I wait in the car?"

"Not at all, baby." Except, after they parked and Gran
got out, Laurel noticed her grandmother hobbling toward
the door, stopping every few seconds to catch her breath.
What the hell?

"Gran?" she said, worried, as she pried herself from behind the wheel and made her own arduous journey over to
the other woman. "What's wrong?"

"No, no…you go back to the car, I'll be okay," she said,
taking another step. Laurel caught her before she crumpled to the ground.

"For heaven's sake! Do you need to see a doctor—?"

"No! I mean, don't be ridiculous. What're they gonna
do, give me a pill for being old? Just help me inside, I'm
sure it'll pass…"

So, slowly, she escorted Gran into the large lobby…only
to notice, through the open doors leading to the poshly appointed gathering room on the other side, not only a whole
lot of people milling about, but a whole lot of balloons and
other party decorations.

A whole lot of *baby boy blue* balloons and party decorations.

"Surprise," Gran whispered behind her.

"This… Wait. It's for me?"

"Since for damn sure nobody here's expecting, yep."

Stunned, Laurel walked closer. Saw tables laden with food. More tables laden with gifts. So many, many gifts. Tears stung as her hand went to her mouth. Her unlipsticked mouth, since, you know, she'd been expecting Gran and Kelly and that was it.

"Hey, everybody!" Gran yelled behind her, making her jump and Jonny thump her bladder. "She's here!"

And out of a rainbow of grinning faces, a gentle roar of applause and welcomes, Kelly appeared, laughing, to pull Laurel into a hug.

"I don't understand...." Her brain still not firing on all cylinders, Laurel edged farther into the room. "How—?"

"Tyler," Kelly said, and Laurel's eyes cut to hers.

"This was *Tyler's* idea?"

"Yep. He said you needed a real party. And since apparently what I had in mind wasn't meeting his exacting standards..." She waved her hand toward the room. "Bam."

"Wait—" Laurel whipped around to Gran. "So your foot—?"

Gran actually cackled. "I'm thinking of a second career as an actress. Whaddya think?"

"So I assume your dishwasher is fine, too."

"Couldn't be better." Grinning, she poked Laurel in the arm. "Are we good, or what?"

Speaking of good... "So where's Tyler?"

Kelly laughed. "It's a baby shower, sweetie. No men allowed. Well, except George over there," she said, nodding toward a blissful-looking, white-haired black gentlemen, who looked to be in the neighborhood of a hundred and fifty.

"Yeah, George goes to everything," Gran said. "Says how else is he going to find his next wife?"

Laurel gawked at her grandmother, then sharply shook

her head. "Well, if George can come, then Tyler can, too."
Digging in her purse for her phone, she edged toward the
breezeway leading from the clubhouse to the pool. "Tell
everyone I'll be there in a sec. They can start in on the
food without me..."

The instant Tyler answered, Laurel's throat clogged. But
she pulled herself together enough to push out, "You get
your butt over here immediately, Tyler Noble! *Capice?*"
Then she ended the call, but not before she heard him laugh.

Which was right around the time she realized her heart
had apparently said "See ya!" to her brain and was mer-
rily skipping down the primrose path.

Oh, no, you don't, she thought, and yanked it right back.

Where it looked up at her, pouting like a petulant child.

If somebody'd told Tyler back in June he'd be spending
this particular Saturday evening helping two women or-
ganize a nursery, he would've wondered what they'd been
smoking. But here he was, shoving piles of freshly washed
baby clothes into drawers and threading a mesh bumper
through the crib's rails and finding someplace to stack
enough diapers, it seemed to him, for ten babies.

It was a little overwhelming, to be honest. And he wasn't
even having the kid. As opposed to Laurel—wedged into
the gliding chair in the corner by the window, both hands
planted on her enormous belly as she wearily told him and
her grandmother where she wanted stuff—who was. And
who still looked like she was gonna cry. Although from
happiness, shock or sheer terror, Tyler wasn't sure. But
then, Laurel probably wasn't, either.

"I can't believe you called those wonderful people—and
I quote, 'a bunch of whining old biddies.' For shame, Gran."

From the other side of the room where she was hanging up the tiniest pair of overalls Tyler had ever seen, Lau-

rel's grandmother shrugged. "Okay, so I might've been wrong about that. Or having a bad day. It happens. But you should've seen them when the van let everybody off at Target—because a lot of 'em, they don't drive anymore, but I couldn't fit everybody in my car—and they all headed straight to the baby department. Like locusts."

She hung up another tiny outfit, a preppie number with a little vest and tie. "But I don't know why you're so surprised, doll. You've always been so sweet to them…why shouldn't they return the favor? Although I don't know if anyone would've thought of it if you hadn't," she said to Tyler, shaking out a little blue snowsuit with Winnie the Pooh on the chest. "That was some great idea you had there. Not only did my baby get the party she deserved, but you gave a lot of old people something to focus on besides themselves. So win-win, right? And now I need to go. I didn't realize it was so late, I don't much like driving after dark these days. Unless you guys still need me—?"

"You go on," Tyler said. "I got this."

"Don't you even try to get up," the old gal said to Laurel as she sidestepped three laundry baskets filled with clean baby duds to lean over and give her granddaughter a hug and kiss. "You look beat. You feel okay?"

"I'm fine," Laurel said with a tired smile. "Just *so* over being pregnant."

"Three weeks?" her grandmother said.

"Not even that. Nineteen days. Eighteen, once we get past midnight."

"Almost there, baby," she said, giving Laurel's hand a squeeze. "You get some sleep, okay? And we'll talk in the morning." Then she turned to Tyler. "You'll keep an eye on her for me, right?"

"Gran, honestly—"

"Absolutely," he said to the or-else expression in front

of him, giving the old gal a little salute before she finally left. "Now tell me how you really feel," Tyler said when he was sure Marian was really gone.

"You have to ask?" Laurel said, letting her head drop back, her eyes drifting shut. "I'm glad you came to the shower."

"Like I had a choice? I half thought if I didn't you'd send a pair of Mafia goons after me. Or your grandmother. Which would've been much worse."

Her eyes still closed, she softly laughed. "True." Then she opened them and said, as she glanced around the room, yawning, "All of this… It makes it seem a lot more real."

"More real than…that?" he said, pointing to her belly, and she smiled, rubbing the mound. Then she pulled the fabric of her shirt taut, watching it rise and fall and twitch. As did Tyler, fascinated.

"Oddly, yes. Go figure." Then she lifted her gaze to him, her smile soft. "I did thank you, didn't I?"

"Several times."

"Oh, God—really? I swear, I'm afraid to go out in public anymore." Her eyes closing again, she snuggled farther back into the cushions, her puffy feet propped on the matching ottoman. "Man, this thing is comfortable. And you should go home. Really. I can deal with the rest of this later. After…a nap…"

And just like that, she was out.

He watched her for a moment, his chest hurting for reasons he couldn't even begin to explain. But he did know he didn't want to leave. Didn't feel like he should, even though he was right next door, right there if she needed him. And that Marian's "order" had nothing to do with it.

Only, that feeling of wanting to stick around, to be with Laurel simply because *he wanted to be with her*… It scared the hell out of him. Because let's be honest—this thing between them, this *friendship*...it was a stopgap thing. Nothing more. For both of them, he imagined. For sure, he'd never go back on any promise he'd made, to her or anybody. But neither did he make promises he couldn't keep.

Which made him wonder, as he finally let himself out and walked back across the front yard to his house, what the hell he'd gotten himself into.

And why.

Hours later, Tyler was having a very bizarre dream involving his being naked in a car wash in the middle of a Blink-182 concert when he realized a) his phone was ringing and b) he was drowning in Boomer slobber. Because Boomer had heard the phone before Tyler did. His heart pounding, he shoved the dog out of his face and fumbled for the phone, dropping it twice before actually getting it to his ear.

"Did I wake you?" Laurel's slightly panicked voice said in his ear.

"No, no—" Tyler did the stretch-your-eyelids-apart-as-far-as-they'll-go thing. "I'm good—"

"So my back was a little achy tonight, right? Like it was before? So I didn't think anything of it? So I went to bed, and everything felt fine...and now I'm standing in Lake Erie. And contrary to what everybody said, my contractions would seem to be coming really, really fast. Also, my crotch feels like it's being blowtorched. So, yeah."

"Wait—you're in labor?"

"Good guess, cowboy." Then her voice changed, to something small and frightened. "How soon can you be here?"

"Three minutes."

"Make it two," she said, and hung up the phone.

Chapter Nine

Moving on pure adrenaline, Tyler shoved the very confused dog out back, pocketed his car keys and booked it to Laurel's. Wearing a nightgown, zipper-front hoodie and the same flip-flops she'd had on earlier, she was already on her porch, bag in hand and clutching a towel. And trembling worse than Boomer in a thunderstorm.

"How far apart—?"

"Five minutes. I c-called my doctor's service. And the hospital. They know we're c-coming. H-here," she said, her keys rattling as she held them out, "we'll take my c-car. In case I get the seat wet."

He decided against reminding her that the truck had leather seats, they were good. Although trying to get her up into it might've been a problem—

She hissed in a breath and terror bit down, hard. *The hell you say,* Tyler thought, smacking it into the next county as he wrapped his arm around Laurel's waist to shepherd her down the steps. He got her settled on her towel in the front seat and zipped around to the driver's side, taking a second to familiarize himself with the dash before backing out into the street, the chirping of one hardy, late-season cricket piercing the thick, predawn silence.

Laurel went very still, staring straight ahead. Tyler shot her what he hoped was a reassuring glance. "How do you—?"

Feel, he was going to ask, but she held up one hand, sharply shaking her head as she coiled into herself, her breathing harsh but steady. Cruising through their neighborhood, Tyler glanced over again, struggling not to flinch at her contorted features. Then she blew out a long breath and seemed to relax. Except for her face, still pinched beneath closed eyes.

Stay cool, stay cool... "Uh...you want some music? To distract you or something?"

Her head jerked again. *No.*

They pulled out on the highway, virtually deserted this time of night. Thank God. "No traffic, like I figured," he said softly. "So ten minutes, tops. You hear that, Jonny? You gotta hang on a little bit longer, okay? Can you do that for your mom?"

That got a soft laugh. "Thank you."

"No problem." He quickly squeezed her arm. "I mean that."

She opened her eyes long enough to give him a brief smile. "I know you do." Her breath hitched. Then she moaned, sending fear streaking through Tyler's veins. "Holy *hell* it hurts..."

"Grab my hand," he said, again reaching across the console.

"No...can't...you're...driving..."

"Got the road to myself... We're okay, honey..."

"Dammit, keep both hands on the wheel!"

He half expected her head to start spinning. Then, again, she released a slow breath. Only this time, when she stopped, he could hear her softly crying. "It wasn't supposed to happen like this. Gran wanted to be there so badly, she..." Laurel knuckled away a tear. "For the last two weeks, that's all she talked about...she was so excited. And now..."

"And now you've got me. At least you didn't have to call a taxi, right? So look on the bright side—"

"Dammit, I *hate* being scared. Hate it, hate it, hate it."

"Hey. If I was about to push a baby out of my body, I'd be scared, too. Not to mention surprised as hell."

That got another laugh. And a little hiccup. "It's not as if I haven't had classes and seen films up the wazoo. I know what's happening. But this is like..." Sucking in another breath, she curled forward, panting.

"Almost there," Tyler said quietly, released a breath of his own when he spotted the brightly lit hospital jutting up alongside the highway. Beside him, Laurel nodded, then wiped at her eyes again, and anger surged through him. That it *shouldn't* have been like this, that it wasn't right...

And maybe, for her sake if nothing else, he should stop dwelling on what wasn't right and focus on what was. Like, for one thing, that he wouldn't be delivering this kid himself.

"The maternity wing entrance is—"

"Got it." He pulled up in front, ran around to help her out. "Can you make it inside, or do I need to get somebody?" She stopped, leaning hard on the fender. "Never mind, I'll be right back—"

Except like magic, an orderly or whatever he was appeared with a wheelchair. Tyler reached into the backseat and grabbed Laurel's bag. "The contractions are coming really fast, we need to hurry…"

Chuckling, the gray-haired black man gently guided Laurel into the chair. "First baby, I take it?"

"Yes," Tyler said, and the man grinned.

"Well, congratulations! Boy or girl?"

"B-boy," Laurel said.

"A boy! A blessing, for sure." The picture of calm, he headed toward the entrance. "You feel like pushing?"

"N-no. Not yet."

"Then you got time," the man said as the automatic doors whooshed open. "Some, anyway."

Tyler scampered behind, the bag getting tangled up in the door for a second. "You sure?"

"Well, nothing's sure in this world—" Now at the nurses' station, the orderly kicked down the wheel lock. "But aside from all the pregnant ladies I've seen come through those doors over the years, I got me six kids of my own. When mama's close to popping? She gets this look on her face—"

"Like that?" Tyler said, nodding toward Laurel as she panted through another contraction.

"Hmm. Close, but not quite. Trust me…you'll know when you see it." He clapped Tyler on the shoulder before sauntering off. "Good luck, Daddy…"

"Oh, I'm—"

"You already in the system, honey?" the admitting nurse, a zaftig brunette with seen-it-all dark eyes, said to Laurel.

"Yes. Laurel Kent. I called a few minutes ago?"

Computer keys clicked, like they were checking into a hotel. "Yep, there you are. You guys are in Room 107, right down the hall." She grinned at Laurel. "Dr. Bernstein's on her way." Then, back at Tyler. "And do you need to go park your car?"

"Oh, right. Yes…I'll…" He looked at Laurel, torn.

The nurse laughed. "First baby, not in transition yet… I think you've got time to park the car. Besides…" Peering through her glasses, she checked the computer monitor. "Looking here at your birth plan…it says here you want an epidural. You still okay with that?"

"God, yes. Is it time?"

"If you're hurting, it's time. So that takes a good twenty minutes," she said to Tyler. "And you can't be in the room. So you may as well go get a cup of coffee, call whoever you need to call." At Tyler's hesitation, she chuckled. "We'll take good care of her, I promise. Now, shoo."

He walked back out to the car, got in behind the wheel. Considering his blood was already surging like river rapids through his veins, coffee was the last thing he wanted. However…

He plucked his phone from his overshirt pocket, tapping two fingers on the steering wheel rim until Marian finally picked up on the fourth ring.

"Tyler…? Ohmigod!" Her gasp bounced off his ear. "The baby's coming?"

"Yep. Just dropped her off at the hospital. Can you be ready in ten minutes? I'll come get you."

"Ten minutes, hell. I'll be ready in five. Pick me up out front!"

"Deal," he said, and drove off, thinking at this rate, he was gonna have to put in an order for tights and a cape.

And maybe a mask, so nobody'd know it was him, doing all this heroic stuff.

"I'm sorry," the labor and delivery nurse—Evonne, her nametag read—said, returning to Laurel's room after the anesthetist left and the hellfire sensation began to subside from her nether regions. Her legs felt kind of numb, too, but ask her if she cared. "Your partner's not out there. Maybe he decided to get something to eat. I'm sure he'll be back soon. How're you doing, baby?"

"Okay," Laurel said, wishing there was an epidural for the brain, to take the edge off the disappointment that Tyler'd left. Heck, for all she knew he didn't even want to be present for the birth. And why should he? But she supposed she'd hoped he'd hang around, at least. If for no other reason than she'd have somebody to show the baby to, after he was born....

"Hey, sweetie," Evonne said softly, wrapping her hand around Laurel's. The woman probably wasn't more than ten years older than she was, but she exuded a motherliness that blanketed Laurel in kindness and warmth. "You still hurting?"

Laurel's jaws clamped together—dammit, her child deserved better than a mother feeling sorry for herself! Blinking, she forced a smile for the nurse, then cocked her head, frowning. "I think…is that a contraction?"

Evonne checked the monitor a few feet from the bed, then smiled for Laurel. "Sure is. Nice long one, too. You'll be ready to push pretty soon—"

Laurel looked up, hopeful, when the door swung open, both grateful and bummed that it was Dr. Bernstein, smiling broadly under a froth of steely gray hair. Laurel had interviewed at least a half dozen doctors before choosing this one, whose direct gaze, easy smile and sense of humor—not to mention decades of experience delivering babies—had put her immediately at ease.

"So little Jonny's decided to jump the gun, huh?" she said, snapping on a rubber glove as she approached the bed.

"Apparently so. I thought I had almost three weeks, yet."

"Yeah, well, babies aren't real good at following timetables. Is your grandmother going to be here for the birth?"

Laurel felt her eyes sting. "That's what we'd planned, but since I went into labor at night…"

"Aw, it'll be okay," the doctor said kindly, squeezing Laurel's hand with her ungloved one. "Let's see what's going on, maybe she can still get here… Can you relax for me…?"

A minute later, the tiny woman peeled off the glove, tossing it in the medical waste bin on the wall as she grinned. "Eight centimeters! Do you have an efficient cervix, or what? And baby's head's right there, ready for launch." The doctor sat on the edge of Laurel's bed, palming her belly, gray eyes twinkling behind frameless glasses. "You excited?"

"Maybe the way I'd be about jumping out of a plane?"

Dr. Bernstein laughed. "Good way of putting it. So I want you to think of Evonne and me as your parachute. Because we're not going anywhere, are we, Evonne?" she tossed over her shoulder.

"Nope," the nurse said. "You picked a good night, baby, nobody else is in labor. Of course, that could change in an hour, but right now? We're golden—"

"All righty…*good* contraction, nice and strong…" The doctor looked at her watch instead of the monitor, smiling for Laurel when she noticed her frown. "The machines have their place, but I'm still old school. I like to be more hands-on." She smiled. "Like the difference between using a bread machine and kneading the old-fashioned way—"

"I'm here, doll baby, I'm here!" In white cotton pants and a patterned blouse Laurel remembered from her childhood, Gran hustled into the room, red lipstick smeared across her mouth. "I look like hell," she said, patting her hair, flattened on one side, "but I'm here."

Her eyes stinging, Laurel smiled. "You do not look like hell, you look like an angel."

Gran grabbed Laurel's hand, pressing it to her soft cheek. "So do you, baby. So do you." Neither one of them would say it, but Laurel could tell from the sheen to her grandmother's eyes that they were both thinking the same thing—that Laurel's mother should be here, too, to greet her first grandchild. How happy she would've been.... "How's she doing, Doc?"

"Fantastic," Dr. Bernstein said. "But I imagine she's doing a lot better now that you're here."

"Gran...how did you—?"

She glanced over her shoulder then huffed a sigh. "Tyler! What the hell are you doing out there? Get in here!" Then she turned to the doctor. "Is that okay?"

"She can have the Knicks in here if she wants...doesn't bother me...."

But whatever the doctor said next, Laurel had no idea. Because all she saw was Tyler, standing in the open doorway, looking so pleased with himself it was ridiculous. "Thanks," she said...a moment before she felt like she was about to lay an egg the size of Newark. Not that she knew what laying an egg felt like, but...

"Tyler!" Gran barked. "The woman needs somebody's hand to squeeze, and better you than me!"

"Uh...you okay with that?" he called over to Laurel, and Gran said, "Oh, for God's sake, she's having a baby, what the hell does she know what she wants? Over here! Now!"

"Welcome to my life," Laurel mumbled, making both the doctor and the nurse chuckle. But then Tyler was there, holding her hand, his gaze locked on hers, his smile almost natural, even...and she let herself believe, for those few precious moments, that he really did want to be right there, with her, witnessing Jonny's entrance into the world.

The next half hour was a blur, of pushing and sweating and grunting, of Gran's "Hot damn!" when Jonny slid out, of the baby being laid on her chest, his little forehead crinkled as he opened his dark blue eyes and looked at her as if to say, "So you're the chick I've been hearing all these months."

And she fell in love so hard it hurt.

"Hey, sweetie," she whispered, laughing and crying at the same time, checking out his spidery fingers and dimpled elbows, his cute little bum and even cuter shell-like ears, before the nurse scrubbed him off and tucked a receiving blanket around him.

"Would you like to cut the cord?" the doctor asked Tyler, and Laurel's eyes shot to his face, his expression every bit as awestruck as hers must have been.

"Ty, you don't have to—"

"Sure," he said with a brief smile…then afterward automatically reached for Jonny when the nurse lifted him off Laurel—how was it possible to already miss him in her arms?—so they could finish up with her.

"Hey, little dude," he said softly, gently rocking the burritoed bundle. "I'm Tyler, your mom's neighbor. You probably recognize my voice, huh? 'Cause your mom and I, we hang out a lot. And this lady," he said, twisting the bundle toward Gran, "is your great-grandmother. She's going to spoil you rotten—"

"Count on it," Gran said, and Tyler grinned at her.

"And those two ladies over there are the doctor who delivered you and the nurse who helped, but they're a little busy right now. You've already met your mom, of course…."

Seeing Tyler so tender and goofy with the baby had already turned Laurel into mush, of course. But now, when he looked over, and she saw how shiny his eyes were, how shaky his smile, she very nearly sobbed out loud. Especially when, blinking rapidly, he veered away, still keeping up the monologue.

"And wait until you see your room," he said as Gran wrapped her fragile hand around Laurel's and held on tight, "and all the clothes and toys and stuff people gave you. You seriously struck gold, dude...."

As he chattered, images came into focus out of the blur...his uncomplaining grasp when she crushed his hand as she pushed, his calm, nonstop encouragement...his gasp of amazement when Jonny appeared, his laugh at the baby's first loud, indignant squawk—

Gran leaned over and whispered, "Seems to me Jonny's not the only one who struck gold, sweetheart," and Laurel thought, *Fool's gold, maybe.*

Because getting caught up in the moment, no matter how sweet, didn't make it real, did it? And as the adrenaline spike began to fade, pragmatism waved in her face and said, *Yo—remember me?*

Sure, Tyler was a sweetheart. No arguments there. But he wasn't *her* sweetheart. And Jonny wasn't his child. And for all his well-meant assurances about his being there for them, how long would that last, really? Because sooner or later some little cutie or other would catch his eye, even if not his heart, and in all likelihood New Girlfriend wouldn't be keen on Tyler's being best buddies with the chick next door. Nor would Laurel blame her. And that was logic talking, not paranoia.

So. Time to gird these loins that had just pushed out an eight-pound baby and get herself back on track. It'd been her decision to do this on her own, and now was not the time to muddy the waters with silly fantasies.

No matter how much she wished she could make those fantasies real.

* * *

In the rush to get Laurel to the hospital, they'd completely forgotten about the car seat. Didn't remember it, either, when Tyler took her grandmother home later that morning to get her own car, when he'd transferred Boomer to Matt's and Kelly's. Who did everything short of congratulating him when he told them about the birth. Because, you know, it wasn't his kid.

Except that feeling of being hit in the head when he'd held Jonny in his arms... Wow. He'd seen all of Ethan's babies soon after they'd arrived, of course, but not right away. And as crazy as he was about his nieces and nephews, he felt very much like an uncle. A little removed, you know?

But Jonny... Holy crap. Like the kid had looked right into Tyler's soul, hooking a line or something between his heart and Ty's.

Now, using the key Laurel'd given him, he let himself into her slightly stuffy, silent house to get the seat, the quiet embracing him like a hug. Her scent, too. Well, not *her* scent, but that unique combination of smells that reminded him of her, of fabric softener and eucalyptus, a whiff of pine from the half-burned Christmas candle on her coffee table.

The car seat was still in its box in the living room, but he felt impelled to check her room, where Jonny would sleep for the first few weeks, make sure the bassinet was ready. But while the white wicker basketlike thing was set up, next to what he assumed was her side of the modest double bed—a simple wood headboard, a plain white comforter with a couple of floral pillows—the tiny mattress was bare. In a drawer in the nursery, he found a sheet that looked like it'd fit, as well as a little quilted pad he assumed went under the sheet, and quickly made it up.

He scanned the room again, spare and neat and soothing in its simplicity, the walls a light, warm beige. Clearly this was someone with no tolerance for clutter, for doodads and tchotchkes and things out of place. He smiled, thinking of Ethan's house, with four kids' stuff scattered all over the place. Of the Nobles' when he lived there, his adoptive mother's enthusiastic support for her children's individual expression—no matter how messy—at constant odds with the Colonel's penchant for regimen and order.

Boy, was Laurel in for a rude awakening, or what? Tyler thought with a smile as he returned to the living room for the car seat, which he quickly installed in her backseat before returning to the hospital. But he kept thinking about how the house felt like Laurel because she'd made it a home. *Her* home. Not simply someplace to eat and sleep and watch TV. Like, say, his place. Even after he'd spruced it up. No surprise there, right? Since how would he know what *home* was?

Seriously, he and his mother had lived so many places he'd eventually stopped trying to remember them all. Most of them were furnished, too, so he never really felt like they were living in *their* house. In contrast, the Nobles were paragons of stability—Tyler had the same room, even the same furniture, from the moment he arrived until he moved out. And yet…he'd never fully felt *at* home there, either. Not nearly as much as he did…

As he did at Laurel's. What the hell?

She was ready to go by the time he got there, looking a little abashed at all the flowers and balloons and crap she'd gotten, mostly from her geriatric groupies at her grandmother's, as well as Kelly and Matt, who'd been by earlier. But after two extra trips from room to car, they finally got all squared away, baby securely strapped into his seat with his mama beside him, and Tyler chauffeured the pair of them back to her house. Her grandmother followed at a not-so-sedate pace behind them, her hair a white cloud in a sea of brightly colored Mylar balloons.

"Seems so weird, doesn't it?" he said. "Go to the hospital with two people, come back with three."

Behind him, Laurel softly laughed. "Weird doesn't even begin to cover it," she said dreamily. But that was it.

She hadn't said a whole lot, actually, since the birth, and Tyler was trying like hell not to let it bug him. Especially since Marian had warned him, when he'd taken her home the day before, that Laurel would be really focused on Jonny for the next little while—that was nature's way of making mothers bond with their babies. Which made perfect sense. To see and hold and touch something that'd been inside you for all those months... What a trip, right? He was hardly going to be jealous of an infant, for crying out loud. Only, he couldn't shake the feeling that Laurel's aloofness—which probably nobody but him could even see—was about more than her being a new mom.

Like her telling him he didn't have to stay at the hospital last night...that he should go home, get some sleep. Anybody else would probably say she was only being considerate, like she always was. So why did he feel that what she was really saying was that she didn't want him around? Or was his own exhaustion making him paranoid?

They arrived without incident, Marian pulling up in Laurel's drive behind them. The old gal was out of her car and up to Laurel's front door in a flash, swinging it open with a huge grin as Tyler carefully scooped a sleeping Jonny from his seat, snuggling him to his chest.

"No, you go on inside," he said softly to Laurel when she tried to take the baby. "You can sit and stare at him the rest of the day if you want."

But this time is mine, he nearly said, the thought going off like a land mine in his brain.

She looked like she might argue, but she didn't. A few minutes later she was settled on the sofa with her son, a tiny frown pushing at her eyebrows. Marian had gone back out to start carting in all the gifts; Tyler squatted in front of Laurel so she'd have to meet his eyes. At least for a moment. "Hey. Talk to me. What's going on?"

At that, a tear slipped over her lower lashes and scurried down her cheek. "It just feels…wrong, that Barry doesn't know his son is here," and another land mine exploded. *Boom.*

Behind him, he heard Marian's gasp, a soft clunk as she set a vase of flowers on the little entryway table. But before Laurel's grandmother could say anything—and Tyler had no doubt she was about to—Laurel looked at him with watery blue eyes and said, "I don't expect you to understand, but…would you mind leaving us alone for a little while? I'm not really feeling much like company right now."

This time, the bomb propelled him to his feet. "*Company?* Seriously?"

"You know what I mean—"

"No, actually, I don't."

She released a shaky sigh. "What you said, about Jonny and me not being alone…that was very sweet. And kind. But we're not your responsibility, Tyler," she said gently. "And I wouldn't dream of burdening you."

Anger surged through him. "And here's a thought— maybe I don't see it that way—"

"Now? No. I'm sure you don't. But what about for the long haul? So if it's eventually only going to be the two of us, anyway…" She pressed her lips together, then said, "I need the space now to figure out how that's going to work. Before…before we get too used to having you around."

He kept their gazes locked for several seconds. Then,

muttering, "Got it," he turned and walked past Marian and out the still-open front door.

"Tyler!" the older woman softly called, catching him before he got down the steps. "Hold on."

Even though talking to Laurel's grandmother was the last thing he wanted to do right then, out of courtesy he waited until she'd quietly closed the door behind her.

"Whatever you're about to say, Marian—"

"You're gonna listen to," she said, her arms folded over her skinny chest. "So suck it up, buster. Look, I have no idea what's going on in your head. Where you're going with this, if anywhere. But I've been around my granddaughter enough to have a pretty good idea what's going on in hers. Even if she doesn't. Because I saw how she looked at you, when you were holding Jonny right after he was born. Saw how much it hurt."

Tyler's brows crashed together. "Hurt? I don't—"

"Because, numbskull, you're being a big tease, dangling something in front of her she wants so badly she can't stand it. Exactly like her father did. Like that schmuck Barry did. God knows I did my best when she was a kid to make it up to her after her father left, to let her know she was loved, *really* loved, that I wasn't going to leave her because maybe things got inconvenient. But I'm eighty-five, for God's sake, I'm not gonna be around forever. So give me one good reason why she should trust that you will be. Or what the hell, I'm not picky, give *her* one good reason. No, seriously, before you open your mouth and spew out what you think I want to hear, think about it. Because that kid I saved from the mouth of hell, she's a grown-up now, and she wants grown-up things. A grown-up relationship, with another grown-up. Not some wannabe thing that's over before it even gets started—"

"Yeah, Marian—I got it," Tyler said, feeling like his

chest was gonna cave in. "You want me to promise forever. You're right…I can't do that. Not like you mean it. Hell, I'm not even sure I fully understand the concept. But I can promise…" Tyler pushed out a breath. "Right *now,* if she needs me, I'm here. Right over there," he said, pointing to his house. "Phone call away. So you tell her that, okay?"

Then he stormed off, madder than he'd been about anything since he was a little kid.

"I don't even want to know what you said to Tyler," Laurel said when Gran found her in the nursery, changing Jonny's tiny diaper.

Gran plopped into the glider. "Sure you do. And I read him the riot act."

Snapping up the baby's sleeper, Laurel frowned at her grandmother. "About what?"

"About how half-assed isn't gonna cut it."

Laurel scooped the baby up off the changing table, carefully cradling him to her aching chest. "So you agree with me."

"In theory? Of course. That doesn't mean he deserved to get kicked out on his ass."

"It's called self-preservation, Gran."

"No, it's called *fear.*"

Laurel met her grandmother's gaze, then shooed her out of the glider before gingerly lowering herself into it, unbuttoning her blouse to put Jonny to breast. "All my life," she said quietly, "I've twisted myself inside out to be accommodating, to understand why somebody didn't or couldn't stick around, couldn't be there for me." She softly grazed the baby's cheek with one finger as he nursed. "And that kept me sane, from getting eaten up alive with resentment. But most of all, learning I could only rely on myself— present company excepted, of course," she said with a slight smile, lifting her eyes to her grandmother, "also kept me from being disappointed."

"So that's why you cut Tyler off."

"You got it."

"Yeah, well, maybe you also cut him off before he was finishing caring—you stop to think about that? Because I've been watching him all these weeks, and trust me, this is not somebody who's gonna screw you and Jonny over. Sure, he's got issues—"

"Ya think?"

"And so do you. So does everybody. And everything you want? You deserve? Same goes for him. But the pair of you... Oh, my God. Too scared and too stubborn to go for it, either of you. And you know something? Before you tell me to stop interfering, I'm outta here. You want so badly to prove you can do this without any help? Go for it, sweetheart."

"Gran—!"

But by the time Laurel struggled out of the chair with the baby still attached to her breast, she heard the front door slam. And except for her own, slightly panicked heartbeat, and Jonny's snuffling, there was absolute silence.

"Guess it's just you and me, sweetie," she whispered to Jonny, trying not to let her voice shake as she settled back in the chair.

Chapter Ten

Zipping up his hoodie against the damp, mid-October breeze, Tyler carted the last of three huge black garbage bags crammed with leaves from *Laurel's* tree he'd spent all afternoon raking up from *his* backyard out to the curb…the very moment her car pulled up in her driveway. He waved, and she waved back—like they always did—but also like always, he didn't know if it was okay to go over there and chat. He did know it was making him nuts, that he had no idea how to fix things between them. Or even what was broken, truthfully.

He'd guessed she and her grandmother had had a blow-out, too, that day they brought the baby home. Because he'd heard Marion drive off, squealing her tires even more than usual. And man, it'd taken everything he had not to call Laurel right then, make sure she was okay. But since she'd made it clear she needed to deal with things on her own, he restrained himself. Especially since he got where she was coming from. Being exactly the same way and all—

"Hey," she said, her voice barely audible over a bunch of brittle leaves skittering down the sidewalk. He took that as encouragement to come closer, only to see her disappear into the backseat.

"Hey, yourself," he said to her denim-covered butt. "Haven't seen you for a while." *Duh.*

She hauled Jonny out of his car seat. Tyler caught a glimpse of fat, pink cheeks protruding from a light blue, pointy hood, little arms and legs like sausages in a puffy, one-piece deal, and that…that *feeling* pinged inside his head. His chest.

"Been a little busy," she said with a smile that looked almost apologetic. Or at least, that's what Tyler was going with. Expertly balancing the baby on her hip, she leaned back into the car to grab a plastic grocery bag, then another…and another…and the diaper bag…

Oh, for crying out loud.

"Here, let me—"

"No, I've got it—"

Ignoring her, Tyler took the bags, giving her a whatcha-gonnadoaboutit? smirk before heading up her stairs. Still balancing the baby—who was sacked out, Tyler noticed—she clumsily unlocked, then pushed open the door, setting Jonny down on the sofa, tummy up, while Tyler marched the groceries back to the kitchen to gently deposit them on the floor…because the counter was too littered with dishes and God knows what else to put them there. Huh.

Then he returned to the living room, which looked like a bomb'd gone off. Stacks of laundry everywhere, mail piled up on the coffee table, even a couple of cobwebs up in the corners, shuddering from the heat coming through the vents.

"Um, thanks," Laurel said, embarrassment coloring her cheeks. Which was when Tyler also noticed the bags under her eyes, the not-so-faint lines bracketing her mouth. "Sorry about the mess. Things've been…well… You know. Anyway—" A smile flickered. "I can take it from here."

"Damn, Laurel—"

"Don't, Tyler. Just…don't. I'm fine, really."

"You don't look fine."

She laughed. "Yeah, sleep deprivation is hell on the looks. I'll live." She crossed her arms. "So…how are things going? Business okay?"

"Uh…yeah, actually." Then he grinned, too proud not to share. "You know those cousins from HGTV? They were apparently working on a house not far from here, so one of their producers scouted out the shop as a potential source for one of their shows…and damned if they didn't use it."

Her face lit up, and Tyler's heart knocked. "Ohmigosh, Ty—that's wonderful! When's it going to be on?"

"Sometime in the spring, they'll let us know the exact date. Can't beat free publicity, right?"

"No, you sure can't." Still smiling, she crossed the room to squeeze his arm. "I'm so happy for you, Ty. Really—"

From the sofa, the baby stirred; Tyler's eyes shot to the infant, his chest doing the same thing it had after the kid's birth. He walked over, looked down. Ached so badly to hold him he thought something would crack inside.

Almost as badly as he ached to hold Jonny's mother. To *really* share his news. Not that everybody else hadn't been happy for him, too—Starla had let out a squeal like he'd announced he was gonna star in a movie—but what he'd seen in Laurel's eyes a second ago…it'd made him *feel* like a movie star. Only better. Sucking in a deep breath, he said, "Man, that is one good-looking kid."

"I think so," she said softly, coming to stand beside him. "But then, I'm not exactly unprejudiced. Um…" Awkwardness settled back between them. "Would you like something to drink? Hot chocolate or tea? Or I think I've got some coffee in the back of the fridge. I could put that on...?"

He thought of that day in June, when they'd first met. How she'd offered him something to drink then, too, not because she really wanted to, but because that's what people like her did. Same as she was doing now. And *poof,* the moment was gone.

For a second, he was tempted to plead to be let back into her life. Except when he looked over and saw that stubborn set to her chin, he thought, *No damn way.* Because it didn't matter what her reasons were for distancing herself from him. If she didn't want him around, she didn't. And hell would freeze over before he'd beg.

"No, that's okay, I gotta... I've got plans."

And if that was disappointment he saw in her bloodshot eyes, too damn bad.

"Of course," she said. "Well. Thanks."

"You bet," he said, and left.

Around two in the morning, though, Dumbbutt Mutt woke him up to go outside. Dragging his robe on over his boxers, Tyler stepped out on his deck, too, yawning as he listened to Boomer nosing around in the dead plants before deciding which one to baptize. The night was clear and cold, so still you could hear your own breathing...still enough to hear—or at least, he thought he heard—a baby wailing next door.

Tensing, he waited, assuming the cries would stop any moment. When they didn't, fear spiked through him, that maybe something was wrong, but Laurel was too proud, or mule-headed, or whatever, to ask for help.

He was dressed and over there in a flash, dog at his side, ringing her bell, then banging on her door—with that crying, he didn't figure there was any danger of waking her up. Finally, after what seemed like forever but was probably less than half a minute, he heard the wails get closer. Then the door swung open…and his heart broke.

Because frankly he wasn't sure who was crying harder, baby or mother.

Boomer shoved up against Tyler, whining in concern. Not even waiting for permission to enter, Tyler shoved past her and the kid, shutting the door. Wearing a pair of what looked like men's pajamas, her hair stringy and tangled, Laurel was bouncing the poor little guy, his scrunched face so red it was practically purple.

"Give him to me," Tyler said, but she shook her head, clinging even harder to the bellowing kid.

"There's n-nothing you c-can do," she said over the pitiful screams. "It's c-colic, his doctor said. He's fed, he's dry, he just…cries, every night, for hours. And I don't know what to *do*—"

Tyler gently clamped both hands around the baby's back and—with no small effort—pried him away from his mother, setting the wailing infant under his own chin. Then, apparently operating on some instinct he didn't even know he had—he'd never been through this with any of Ethan's brood—he started pacing the living room.

"Go back to bed, honey."

"I c-can't do that—!"

"You've gotta get some rest or you're not gonna be any good to him. So go. Now. No arguments."

"I'll never be able to sleep—"

Jonny paused, hauled in a shaky breath, then screamed so loud Tyler's brain rattled. Worried, Boomer stood on his hind legs, his front paws propped on Tyler's arm like he was thinking, *Dude, what the hell is* wrong *with that thing?* Tyler nailed Laurel with his gaze.

"It's like this either you go to bed now, or I hand him

back to you, walk out that door and never come back. So what's it gonna be?"

She looked at her squalling baby, then back at Tyler. "He'll need to eat again in a couple of hours—"

"Then I will bring him to you."

Finally, she stepped closer to briefly rub Jonny's back, then practically ran from the room, shutting her bedroom door behind her.

And Tyler and the dog settled in for probably the longest night of their lives.

Laurel awoke with a panicked start, her head groggy, her breasts full. She glanced at the clock: Nearly *seven?* What the—?

She stumbled to the bathroom to pee, quickly drag a comb through her tangled hair. Then she scurried to the living room, where she found, illuminated by a single lamp left on beside the sofa, Tyler sacked out on her grandfather's old La-Z-Boy recliner with a snoozing, fuzzy-headed Jonny splayed across his chest, both of them with their mouths sagged open. Boomer, stretched out beside the recliner, lifted his head to give her his goofy grin, his stubby tail wagging. Across from them, a pair of ridiculously chipper TV hosts bantered with each other. Laurel grabbed the remote and clicked off the TV, then looked down at the pair of sleeping beauties, her eyes filling.

Damn you, Tyler Noble.

How long the baby had cried, she had no idea. Having passed *exhausted* at least two weeks ago, she'd crashed like she'd been drugged as soon as her head hit pillow. So much for *don't need no stinking help from nobody.*

As if he could smell the milk beginning to leak from her swollen breasts, Jonny stirred, then let out a tiny, wrinkle-faced squawk. Tyler instantly snapped to attention, his hands tightening around the baby as he blearily met Laurel's gaze. Boomer scrambled to his feet to give his daddy, then the baby, sloppy doggy kisses.

"Good morning," she whispered, taking Jonny and settling into the sofa, putting him to breast without bothering to check his diaper. The dog jumped up beside her to keep tabs on the proceedings, laying his jowly head on her knee. Tyler righted the recliner, blinking at them for several seconds before releasing a huge yawn. Laurel almost smiled—his hair, sticking out in a thousand directions, looked worse than hers. Although at least she didn't have beard stubble. Small mercies.

"You said something about coffee?" he said, then frowned. "Yesterday?"

"Go for it."

He seemed to take a moment to gather his wits before pushing himself out of the chair, making his own bathroom pit stop before ambling to the kitchen, stretching and popping his spine as he walked.

"You sleep?" he called from the kitchen.

"Like the dead." She paused, then said, stroking Jonny's pulsing soft spot as he guzzled, "Thank you."

"No problem." She heard some rattling and clunking, the sound of water running. Minutes later the smell of coffee filled the house.

"Want a cup?"

"Not me, no. Nursing." She paused. "But if you wouldn't mind pouring me some orange juice…?"

"Coming right up."

He appeared almost immediately with a huge glass of juice, which she took with another shy "Thanks," drinking as greedily of it as the baby did from her. Tyler nodded then returned to the kitchen. "How…how long did he cry after I went to bed?"

"Dunno. Although, for future reference? He really digs The Weather Channel."

"I'll keep that in mind," she said, smiling, as Tyler reappeared with his coffee. Shaking his head at the dog, he sat forward on the edge of the recliner, the mug cupped in his hands as he watched the baby.

"He really cries every night like that?"

"For the last week or so, yeah."

"So how come I never heard him before?"

"Because it's cold enough that everyone has their windows closed? His doctor swears he'll outgrow it, but…" She shrugged. "It's what I signed up for, so I can't really complain."

Tyler lifted his mug to his lips, taking a long sip before saying, very quietly, "Is it? What you signed up for?"

Laurel paused, then said, "We only have control over our choices. Over the consequences of those choices, not so much." Jonny's suckling became less frantic as his tummy filled; Laurel took the opportunity to gently detach him from the nipple and lift him to her collarbone, rubbing between his shoulder blades until he belched so loudly he startled himself, little hands flailing.

"Impressive," Tyler said, and Laurel smiled, switching the baby to the other side as discreetly as possible. Then she lifted her eyes to Tyler.

"We've also been granted," she said softly, "the grace to admit when we're wrong."

His gaze bored into hers. "Oh, yeah?"

"Not that I didn't need to *try* doing this alone. Well, mostly—Gran does help, when she can—"

"So you two made up?"

Laurel smiled. "As if she could stay away from her great-grandson for long. But she's been dealing with a stubborn cold the past couple weeks, so she didn't feel right about coming over." A short laugh preceded, "Hence the mess. Look—I still don't dare let myself lean too heavily on other people. That's just foolish. But…what's more foolish is not accepting help when it's offered."

"No argument here."

Her mouth twisted. "Unfortunately, there's a very fine line between self-preservation and pride. And for my child's sake…" She sighed. "What's best for me isn't necessarily what's best for him. I can take care of myself, sure. He can't. And if I'm too wiped out *to* take care of him…what then? So," she said, looking down at her precious, precious baby, "this is me…letting go. Admitting how close I was to losing it last night…" Her gaze lifted again to Tyler's. "As well as how incredibly grateful I am that you came to my rescue."

A long pause preceded "This mean we're good again?" and her heart turned inside out.

We *were never not good,* she thought. But all she said was, "Yeah. We're good."

His cheeks actually puffed with the force of his sigh before he got to his feet. "Okay, then." One hand curved around the back of his neck as apology swam in his eyes. "I need to get cleaned up, head to work… Will you be okay?"

Laurel smiled. "You kidding? I got more than four hours sleep in one stretch last night. I'm ready to run a marathon. Anyway, Gran's coming over later… She's finally better. So we'll be fine."

He called the dog, who rolled his eyes up to Laurel, as though pleading with her to stay. "Boomer! Come on, she doesn't need to deal with you on top of everything else. But we'll be back—" Tyler's eyes cut to hers. "We will, won't we?"

"Anytime you want."

"You sure?"

"Positive," she said, and he grinned. The dog finally slid off the sofa and trudged behind Tyler to the door. Where he turned, one hand on the door's edge, and said, "I really missed you."

"Yeah. Me, too."

Then they were gone. Babykins finally done with his breakfast, Laurel shoved up off the sofa and carted the sleeping infant to the nursery, where she changed his diaper and laid him on his back in his crib. For several moments, she watched him sleep, his delicate fingers curled around one of hers, loving him so much she could barely breathe.

Heaven knows her life wasn't going the way she'd expected. Or hoped. Maybe it never would. But letting go, letting Tyler back *into* her life, and her child's…she couldn't even begin to put into words the feelings of peace, of rightness, buoying her right then. To reject Tyler because he couldn't be what she wanted, instead of being grateful for what he was… To be afraid of something that hadn't even happened…

Idiot.

The baby snuffled in his sleep, a tiny bubble of milk cresting, then popping, in the corner of his little cupid mouth, and Laurel smiled. Right now, things *were* good. Right now she had a healthy, sleeping baby with a full tummy, and almost five hours of uninterrupted sleep under her belt, and Gran would be over in a bit and Laurel was going to soak in the tub for twenty whole minutes….

And she and Tyler were friends again.

For now, that was enough.

Over the next couple of weeks, Tyler and Laurel settled into something like a routine, where he'd go over to her place after work several nights a week, and sometimes he'd bring pizza or Chinese food, or Laurel would heat up some dish or other that Kelly—who'd announced her own pregnancy with much hugging and squealing the week before—had donated to the cause. Or sometimes, now that Jonny's colic was easing up and Laurel wasn't quite as frazzled, she'd cook. After a fashion. God knows her heart was in the right place, but Tyler wasn't all that sure the kitchen was it.

And on Sundays, since he'd had to work most Saturdays recently, what with people trying to finish up renovation projects before the real cold weather hit, they'd go over to Matt and Kelly's, or bundle up the kid and take Marian out to eat. Almost like they were a real family.

Almost being the operative word, here.

He'd meant it about missing Laurel. So being part of her life again made Tyler feel good about *his* life in a way he hadn't in a very long time. If ever. Like maybe, for once, he was on the right track. Or at least he could see the right track. But that *almost*...

A word that pretty much described his existence up to that point, didn't it? Or at least his relationships, he thought as he crossed the frost-crunchy grass the Sunday before Halloween to get to Laurel's. Like he was *almost* somebody's son, or somebody's brother...or somebody's boyfriend. Only more and more he was beginning to think that *almost* wasn't cutting it. Even if he had no clue how to upgrade to...to whatever came after *almost*.

Or even if he could.

But right now they needed to deal with grocery shopping. Not that Laurel wasn't perfectly capable of juggling the kid and the stuff and the car—as she so often reminded him—but she did admit it was easier with him along. Easier for her, at least bearable for him, since grocery shopping ranked pretty low on his favorite-things-to-do list. Except today—not that Laurel knew this yet—they were going to buy a buttload of candy to hand out to trick-or-treaters, and a pumpkin or two to carve, and maybe swing by Target or Walmart or someplace and buy a bunch of junk to decorate their yards with. Webs and spooky lights and quite possibly one of those crazy inflatable things, a ghost or giant pumpkin or something—

He'd just knocked on Laurel's door when his phone rang. Frowning at Starla's number in the display, he answered, holding up one finger when Laurel opened her door. Jonny was dressed in his snowsuit—it was frickin' freezing today—with a pumpkin costume over it. Hysterical.

"Yeah?" he said into the phone.

"Sorry to bother you, and you know I wouldn't if I had any other choice…but I've got a flat and I need to be at work in twenty minutes. Could you *possibly* give me a lift? I'll pay for the gas—"

"You don't need to pay for the gas, but…hold on." He put the phone on mute, then said to Laurel as she locked her door, "Emergency. Starla needs a lift to work. You want me to come back later?"

She gave him a brief, weird look then shook her head. "No, Jonny's finally gotten into a good afternoon nap routine. No way am I disrupting that. Better if we tag along."

"You don't mind?"

"Of course not," she said, starting toward her car. "But let's get going."

"Be right there," Tyler told Starla, then pocketed his phone to take the baby from Laurel to put him in his car seat. Not that *she* couldn't, but that wasn't the issue. The issue was—the kid gave him a wobbly grin—*this*.

He couldn't quite believe it, either, how attached he'd gotten to the little twerp. But there it was. And here *he* was. As opposed to Barry, who was still MIA.

"You still haven't said how you know Starla," Laurel

said when they got going, looking straight ahead as Jonny occasionally cooed in his car seat behind them.

Yeah. This again. Tyler shifted in his seat—Laurel insisted on driving when they took her car, and, yes, it drove him nuts, even though she was probably a better driver than he was. "From when I was a kid," he said. "Before the Nobles adopted me."

"Like…a friend of the family?"

"Sure," he said, not daring to look at her. "I hadn't seen her for a long time, when we ran into each other again a few years ago. In Costco, in fact, when I was there with Abby, picking up some supplies for the shop."

Every bit of it was true, including his spotting Starla three registers over from where they were checking out, that day two years ago. What he didn't say, of course, was how his belly had felt like it'd caught fire when he'd recognized her. That it'd taken him another month before he went back, made contact. Her scream of joy when she realized it was him.

What he *couldn't* say, didn't fully understand, was why he still didn't feel comfortable telling Laurel who Starla really was. Especially since, now having some hands-on experience himself with caring for a newborn, the pain of his mother's abandonment had begun to loosen its grip, giving way to a weird blend of empathy and—here's where things got dicey—shame.

Yeah, at first maybe he'd resisted coming clean to Laurel because they weren't close, so his personal life, his past, had been none of her concern. But now that they were friends it mattered what she thought—about him, his choices. So to admit the truth also meant owning up to what a hardass he'd been all these years. Tyler could only imagine the look she'd give him, when she found out—

"So…that's when you resumed your relationship?" she said, her words slicing through his thoughts.

"I think *relationship* might be pushing it," he said, daring to toss her a smile. "*Acquaintance* is more like it."

"You build walls for everybody you're acquainted with?"

She was teasing, he knew that. But the inadvertent double meaning to her words hit him upside the head. "Hey. I built one for you. And we'd barely said hello to each other."

"That wall was to keep *your* dog out of *my* yard. Or rather, to keep him in yours. So. Not entirely altruistic."

He grinned again, even though by this point his stomach was roiling. Starla was waiting in her driveway, the world's ugliest parka thrown on over her jeans. Maybe he'd take her shopping, get her a new coat for Christmas—

She was thrilled out of her gourd, of course, getting to see the baby. And she insisted on sitting in back beside him. Tyler knew she'd never expose their secret, if for no other reason than she'd said herself, she'd given up any right to call herself his mother years ago. A thought that now made him cringe.

"I *thought* you were pregnant when you came out to the house before," Starla said in her squeaky-rough voice. "Ohmigosh, he's beautiful! What's his name?"

"Jonathon. Jonny."

"Well, hello, Jonny! Ohmigosh, look at that! He smiled at me!"

Laurel laughed. "He just started that about a week ago."

"Those gummy little smiles are the best," Starla said, laughing as well…but Tyler heard the regret, as well. Or maybe he imagined it. After all, she'd seen his first smile, heard his first laugh. But…had he been colicky, too? Had she spent hours walking him trying to get him to stop crying? With no one to relieve her—?

"You have kids, Starla?" Laurel asked, and Tyler's heart knocked.

The briefest beat preceded, "One. A son. He's all grown-up now, of course. But I remember when he was a baby like it was yesterday."

"Do you see him often?"

"From time to time," she said softly. "We're...not particularly close."

"Oh...that's too bad," Laurel said, as Tyler's chest cramped so hard he could barely breathe.

"Yeah," Starla said. "It is. But I still have hope that we'll sort out our differences one day. Because without hope, might as well die, right?"

"Absolutely," Laurel said, her gaze fixed out the windshield. "I'll hope along with you, how's that?"

"Aw, you're a real sweetheart, you know that? Tyler told me you're a single mom, too. Like I was."

Laurel shot Tyler a glance, then refocused on the road. "Jonny's dad's not in the picture, no. But I've got my grandmother. And this guy next to me..." She smiled. "He's been a huge help. Once I got over myself and *let* him help me, anyway."

"Oh, yeah? Isn't that nice."

"It is." Spotting the entrance to the Costco parking lot, Laurel smoothly pulled into the exit lane. "He's going to be a really good daddy someday."

"I don't doubt it for a minute," Starla said, and Tyler wanted to say, *Hello? Sitting right here?*

They pulled up alongside the warehouse club's entrance; Starla got out, calling back into the car before she shut the door, "Give that baby lots and lots of kisses for me, okay?"

Then, with a cheerful wave, she scooted into the store, and Tyler released a long, silent breath, that at least that was over. Only to nearly choke when Laurel said, "We should have her over for dinner sometime."

"What?"

"Why not? You said you'd known her since you were a kid, right? And I bet she'd love to hang out with Jonny."

"I'm…sure she would—"

"I mean, this would be totally up to her, but…Jonny could use a grandmother figure in his life."

"Aside from yours, you mean?"

"Gran's *my* grandmother. Not Jonny's. And…" When she hesitated again, Tyler glanced over to see a small, sad smile curving her lips. "Sometimes, it absolutely rips me up inside, that my own mother will never know Jonny."

"And you think Starla could fill the gap?"

He hoped to hell that hadn't come out as harsh as it sounded in his head, because he hadn't meant it to. Because, weirdly, he got where she was coming from—that if major players were missing from your own family, what was wrong with piecing one together from scraps of other people's?

"No," she said, surprising him. "Not for me, anyway. Or Gran. Starla's a sweetie, but she can't replace my mother. But maybe… I don't know." Her eyes briefly cut to his, then away. "Jonny and I could fill a gap in *Starla's* life?"

Not for the first time, Tyler wondered at the apparent disconnect between Laurel's practical nature and her big heart. And yet, to her, more or less "adopting" Starla, thereby meeting a mutual need, probably made perfect sense.

To her, anyway.

"So…you'll ask her? Maybe for sometime next week?"

"Sure," he said, and she might've rolled her eyes, he couldn't quite tell. Although at least she dropped the subject. But what else was he gonna say? Because "Let me think about it," or worse, a flat-out "no," would have only raised flags.

Flags that kept flapping in his own face, anyway, when Laurel got real quiet again as they shopped. That still fluttered hours later as Laurel fixed dinner for them while he put up the few Halloween decorations they'd found cowering in a back corner in Target's Seasonal department, already burgeoning with Christmas crap. But they did have pumpkins, oh, yeah. And they'd bought enough Halloween candy to keep every dentist in Jersey busy for years—

They.

Them.

In the midst of stringing a set of skeleton lights across Laurel's porch, Tyler stopped, listening to the words dance through his brain.

We...

Us...

And, once again*, almost.*

He remembered that morning after he'd stayed up with Jonny, and he'd awakened to find Laurel standing there, all pink and sleep-creased and rumpled, so tender-eyed when she'd looked at her sleeping baby his heart had practically jumped into his throat...and she'd turned that gaze on him, like he was her savior or something, and...

Hell.

His fingers nearly frozen by now, he plugged in the lights, the soft purple glow appropriately spooky, especially when blurred by wisps of that webbing stuff he'd stretched all over the porch. It wasn't nearly as awesome as he'd seen it in his head, but there was always next year—

His throat clogged.

Next year?

He knocked on the window—Laurel hadn't pulled the blinds shut yet—gesturing for her to come outside. A moment later, wrapped up in that same big shirt she'd been wearing when they'd first talked—hell, yeah, he remembered—she joined him, her lips barely tilted as she touched a hunk of web, floating like a fake-spider-infested glob of cotton candy.

"This is really cool," she said, sounding a little subdued, a little sad.

And Tyler heard, like the words were coming out of somebody else's mouth, "I think we should get married."

Chapter Eleven

Laurel didn't know whether to laugh or stick a sharp object in her eye. Or shove Tyler over the porch railing. As it was, all afternoon she'd been swallowing down her frustration with his refusal to admit Starla was his birth mother—about which, after that conversation with the woman in her car, she now had no doubt. Then he does *this?* Good God.

"*What* did you say?"

He looked a little ill—although, granted, that might've been from the purple lights—but damned if he didn't say it again. "We should get married. Hey," he said when she laughed, "you're the one who keeps harping on what makes the most sense. What's *practical.*"

"For whom, Tyler? Especially since you've made it plain enough you don't even want marriage and family—"

"So, what? I can't change my mind?"

Lord love a duck, the man had lost his marbles. And she was freezing. Not to mention still mad about the other thing. Which, actually, she'd planned on confronting him about after dinner. Also, probably heartbroken, but at this point that was so far down the list she couldn't even see it, let alone react. Shaking her head, Laurel went back inside, half hoping Tyler would stay out until the cold air cleared the craziness from his brain.

No such luck.

"And anyway," he said, following her and shutting the door behind him, "this isn't about me…it's about Jonny. And…you. What you said earlier, about piecing together a family—"

"And I just went from flabbergasted to pissed," she whispered so she wouldn't wake Jonny, asleep in his swing. Then she tramped back to the kitchen, where she was attempting to duplicate Kelly's spaghetti and meatballs. Boomer lifted his head then heaved himself to his feet, plodding back to the living room to collapse by the swing.

"This isn't exactly going the way I'd hoped it would," Tyler said behind Laurel from the kitchen doorway.

"Oh, no?" she said, the sauce splattering everywhere as she stirred. He came closer, removing the spoon from her hand and setting it down. Then he turned her around to tuck her against his chest, holding her close. You know, like a brother. Or something.

"I'm sorry," he said, and she sighed.

"Where is this coming from, Tyler?" she said, pulling away. "I mean, really?"

He streaked a hand through his hair then pointed to the porch. "I was out there, after I put up everything, all right? And it's not everything I hoped it would be, it's kinda lame, actually, but I thought, well, there's always next year…." His hand dropped. "And then I thought, what if there isn't a next year? For us, I mean. And I felt like I needed to *do* something. So I wouldn't lose this. So *we* wouldn't."

Oh, dear God. Kill her now, why not?

"And what, exactly," Laurel said gently, "are you afraid you'll lose?"

His mouth pulled taut before he rammed his fingers into his pockets. "Feeling like…like I'm part of something. Something I had a hand in putting together, I mean. Not something I was thrown into."

Her eyes stung. "And you won't lose my friendship. I promise. But marriage…" She swallowed, refusing to cry. Keeping the flush from sweeping up her neck and face, however, was something else again. "You don't love me, Ty."

His eyes lowered. "Maybe not in the traditional sense, but—"

"Tyler. Please. Maybe you're willing to settle for 'good enough,' but I'm not." She paused, feeling her face heat again. "Not with someone I'd be sharing a bed with."

One side of his mouth lifted. "Yeah, your grandmother said something about you being picky."

"After what I just went through? You betcha." She exhaled sharply. "Look…heaven knows I'm no expert on marriage, but I've witnessed firsthand the difference between a union that was really a *union,* and one that hobbled along for a dozen years using obligation as its crutch. I refuse to follow my parents' example, refuse to do to Jonathon what they did to me—"

"Except if it's my idea, how would this be about obligation?"

"Because you're not the kind of person who breaks his promises. And I wouldn't dream of trapping you in something I don't think you've thought through. Living in a loveless house sucks."

"This wouldn't be like that, I swear—"

"Tyler." Laurel curled her hands around his biceps to

look him straight in the eye. Whether he was ready to come clean or not, it was time she did. For everybody's sake. "When you realized Jonny might not ever meet, let alone know, his father…that really struck home, didn't it? Because you never knew who your father was. Then your mother let the Nobles adopt you—"

"How do you know about that?" he said, looking like he'd been sucker punched, before he loudly exhaled. "Kelly. Right?"

"She thinks the world of you, you know," she said quietly. "They all do. Because they're your *family.*" She gave his arms a quick squeeze, then folded her own across her stomach. "But this out-of-the-blue proposal… What comes to me, is that you're seeing Jonny and me as some kind of compensation for whatever you feel you've missed in your own life—"

"What? No—"

"And that somehow this is tied in with Starla's giving you up."

Tyler froze, his eyes boring into hers, before, with a muttered curse, he walked out of the kitchen. Laurel found him perched on the edge of the recliner, his head in his hands.

"If you knew," he said, dropping his hands but not looking at her, "why didn't you say something before?"

"Because—here's a thought—maybe I was hoping you'd tell me yourself? Seriously, Ty…don't you think this is kind of major stuff to keep from someone you ask to marry you? Kelly shouldn't have had to tell me anything. And I shouldn't have had to guess about Starla—"

"So maybe I didn't want to burden you with my crap," he said, his eyes finally meeting hers.

"You mean, the crap you've been lugging around with you since you were a little kid? The crap everybody who's ever known you can smell a mile away?"

He almost smiled. "You are something else, you know that?"

"Yeah. I do, actually. Meaning I can handle the crap. Share the burden. You know, like couples are supposed to? But clearly you're not there. Not yet—"

"I want to take care of you, Laurel!" he said, surging to his feet again. "You and Jonathon!" His gaze veered to the baby, sweetly oblivious to the goings-on, before returning to Laurel. "Look, it's not like I don't know how everybody thinks I'm just some big kid, that I missed the bus when they boarded for adulthood. So here I am, ready and willing—"

"To take care of us. Got it. Setting aside the issue that, hey, maybe that's not exactly what I had in mind for a marriage proposal, perhaps I also have a different take on what it means to be responsible. To be an adult."

"What's that supposed to mean?"

Laurel sat on the sofa in front of a mountain of clean baby clothes, sorting them as she tried to sort her thoughts. "Okay," she said, holding a little sleeper dotted with tiny Tiggers to her chest, "when my father basically abandoned me after my mother died, I couldn't shake the hurt." She folded the sleeper, set it on a pile with a half dozen others. "Like…I'd been slapped, but the sting wouldn't go away. But I felt so…*justified* in hating him—and believe me, I did, for a long time—that even the idea of letting it all go felt wrong."

Tyler gave her a brief, hard stare, then turned away to stand in front of her picture window, where, outside, everything glowed a soft, eerie purple. Laurel folded the last sleeper then started in on a tangle of receiving blankets. "I didn't talk about it a lot, but Gran knew, of course. And one day she said—very casually—something about how hard it is to fully love if even *part* of your heart is all wrinkled and black with resentment."

Tyler was silent for several beats then grunted in that way a man does when he doesn't want to admit someone else might be right.

"Of course, being a stubborn teenager by then, I was convinced Gran was talking through her hat. Until one day, well after the worst of the grief should have been long over, I realized…I wanted to be happy again. And that I never would be unless I changed my thinking. Since I obviously couldn't change my father's."

"So, what?" Tyler turned, glowering at her. "You forgave him, just like that?"

"Of course not. But I did decide that whether or not I was happy was my choice. Not his."

He turned back to the window. "Like you did with Barry."

"Pretty much, yeah," she said, imagining the tussle he and his pride were having right about now. "Because it was either that or spend the rest of my life miserable." When he didn't reply, she said, "Ty, I'm not telling you what to do. That's not my place, even if I could. But whatever you need to work out with your mother, about your childhood, can't be sidestepped by faking something with me and Jonathon. By…by trying to take Barry's place. It won't work—"

"Yeah, well," he said, wheeling on her, "epiphanies aren't one size fits all, are they? Your mother died, and that sucks, and your father dumped you on your grandmother…but at least you knew who he was. He wasn't some secret to apparently be kept at all costs. And your mother didn't give you up because her habit was more important than her kid. Or let some other family adopt you even *after* she was clean. Or tell you *why* she did that, no matter how many times you ask—"

Tyler faced the window again, but she could see his Adam's apple work overtime as he desperately tried to keep his emotions in check. And she hurt so much for him she could barely breathe. Especially since she knew what he'd sacrificed, opening up to her like this: not only that pride, but whatever wall he'd built around himself, however flimsy, to keep the pain from destroying him completely.

Then, on a long sigh, he cupped the back of his neck. "What I feel for you," he said softly, "for Jonathon...it's not fake. That much I can tell you. Maybe you're right, maybe it's not enough...but it sure as hell is real. As real as I can make it, anyway. I'm not trying to take anybody's place. I'm trying to find my own."

"I know," she whispered. "I really do—"

"I'd be good to you," he said, turning, his throat working again. "I'd never hurt you. Or leave you. I swear."

His plea nearly destroyed her. Because nobody understood more than she did his longing for a real family, a *complete* family, even if he'd been in denial about that for so long. True, he'd had a damn good approximation of that with the Nobles—whether he could admit that or not— same as she'd had with Gran. But it wasn't the same as, well, what they'd both lost. If they'd ever really had it. And his willingness to sacrifice his autonomy only made her...

Only made her love him more.

Except...

"I know that, too. But you still don't love me. Not the way I want—no, *deserve*—to be loved."

Laurel felt as though she could have written several pages of her next book before he finally muttered, "Not sure I even know what that is."

"Don't know?" she said gently. "Or afraid to let go enough to find out?"

Another long pause preceded, "Does it matter?"

Her eyes stinging, Laurel stood and went to him, threading her arms around his waist. "You are one of the most honorable men I've ever known," she said softly. "And you have no idea how much it's tearing me up inside to turn you down. Your goodness isn't the issue. It never was. But I honestly don't believe you're in the right place to take on a ready-made family, no matter how well intentioned your motives. And in the long run, I don't think any of us would be happy."

His tortured gaze bored into hers. "In other words, you don't think I'm mature enough for you."

"I don't think you're *whole* enough." She palmed the center of his pounding chest. "In here. Big difference." Letting go, she slipped her hands into her back pockets. "Jonny and I…we can't fix you. Only you can do that."

They stood together for several seconds, gazes locked, before, on a long breath, Tyler nodded. Then, after pressing a light kiss to the top of her head, he walked to the front door and let himself out, just as Jonny's little jungle bird squawk from the swing snagged Laurel's attention.

Scrubbing tears off her cheeks, Laurel scooped up her burbling son to hold him close, letting his sweet warmth soothe her mangled heart.

A chilly, light mist had begun to sheen Tyler's skin by the time he and a panting Boomer sprinted onto the Colonel's street, which was dotted with the occasional Halloween remnant—a crumpled pumpkin, a wisp of webbing. His legs and lungs burned, but it was a good burn, the kind that seared not only his limbs but hopefully his brain. At least enough to keep him from getting into it with the old man. For once.

He'd probably wanted to ask for Tyler's help less than Tyler wanted to go over there. Because he'd been the last choice. And God knows Tyler, left to his own devices, would probably be sitting in the dark, chugging a beer and listening to the most morose, mind-numbing music he could dredge from his playlist.

Real mature, he knew. But you know what? Tough. Because—not that Laurel had actually said this, but he wasn't a total idiot, he could read between the lines—maybe he never would grow up, maybe this was as up as he was ever gonna get, dating bubbleheaded blondes and running in the damn rain with his damn dog, until their bodies gave out and they were reduced to lumps on his sofa, watching crap-ola TV until their heads exploded. Well, Tyler's, anyway.

Except that'd already happened, hadn't it?

A cat scurried across the street; the dog jerked on his leash, practically wrenching Tyler's arm out of the socket.

"Forget it," Tyler huffed out, yanking the dog back. "No sense going after things you can't get."

Yeah. That.

Seriously—what'd he been thinking, blindsiding Laurel like that? Not to mention himself? *When* was he gonna learn to think things through instead of just going with the moment?

Maybe he didn't want to know the answer to that.

Panting as bad as the dog, Tyler pounded up the porch steps to the elegant Queen Anne, slicking rain off his hair before digging his old house keys from his sweatpants pocket, letting himself in. Boomer dashed to the kitchen and the automatic water dish always available for visiting granddogs.

"Pop?"

Funny how even after all this time, the name still didn't sit right in Tyler's mouth. Never mind that the Colonel had more than plugged up that hole in Tyler's life for nearly twenty years. Tried to, anyway.

"Family room!"

Tyler followed the old man's voice to the paneled room off the kitchen, where, as a kid, Tyler'd spent many an afternoon watching Power Rangers cartoons. Then, later, Saturday mornings watching *This Old House* and HGTV remodeling shows, earning him many a "Seriously? Again?" from his older siblings. This room, however, was about as far from HGTV-worthy as it got, the paneling dull, the leather furniture saggy and scuffed, the carpeting worn—the hallmarks of a space where, for a decade or so, a bunch of kids had found "family" right when the concept had seemed most out of reach. Now, stacked with military precision in front of the bare, built-in bookcases smothering one side of the room, were dozens of cardboard boxes. Presumably filled with the hundreds of books that used to live on those bookcases.

Children's books. The classics. Jeanne's vast collection of paperbacks, spanning every genre imaginable. A shrine, Tyler now realized, to a woman's intense love of reading, of learning. Of sharing.

His gaze swung to his father, taping up one of the boxes, and something inside him twinged.

"What's going on?"

"Library said they'll take the whole lot if we can get 'em there. Can't lug 'em all out to the truck by myself, though. Back's not what it used to be. This getting old business is for the birds—"

"And why are you getting rid of the books?"

"Nobody's touched them in years, Ethan's kids all use those tablets or e-readers or whatever they are." He straightened, pressing his knuckles into his lower spine. "And the Realtor said the place was way too cluttered, anyway—"

"Wait. Realtor? You're selling the house?"

"Hand me that roll of tape, would you? Over there on

the wet bar. Yeah, I'm finally ready to let go of it. To blast myself out of the past. Thanks," he said, taking the roll from Tyler, then wedging it into the dispenser before turning to the next box.

"I don't..." His forehead cramped. "Why now?"

The old man frowned toward the backyard, then bent to tape the next box. "Because the other day I was out looking at Jeannie's rosebushes, thinking about how I'll have to prune them come spring, and it's like something clobbered me on the back of my head, that I was only hanging on to the place because as long as I did Jeannie was still with me." The tape *wrrratched* across the box. "And I realized that rosebushes, books, the house...those aren't Jeannie." He slicked the heel of his hand across the tape, moved to the next box. "Never were...never will be. So I'm selling. Clearing it all out, unless you kids want any of it."

Whoa. This was...epic. "And...then what?"

"That Marian, who was here with Laurel for the wedding? She was talking about how much she loves where she is, so I checked it out. And I think that'll suit me fine. Especially since Abby's taking over Matt's basement apartment."

"But..." Tyler dropped onto the edge of his father's wobbly recliner, not sure which was messing with his head more—the subject of the conversation or that they were actually having one. Shooting the breeze had never been their thing. "You love this house."

"Loved. Past tense. And what it represented a lot more than the place itself. Hell, it was our first real home, after all those years of base housing, of moving every five minutes. Watching Jeannie finally getting a place to decorate any way she wanted... It was great, no doubt about it. But that period of my life...it's over. Jeannie's gone...you guys are all grown..."

He stopped, blinking for a second before meeting Tyler's gaze again. "We'd planned on growing old here. But that didn't happen. And wishing things were different, ruminating about the past like that's going to somehow change things? Huge waste of time."

"Still. It seems so...out of the blue."

"Truthfully, I think it's been in the back of my mind for years. Even if it took a while to work to the surface." Behind his glasses, his eyebrows bunched. "And what's it to you, anyway? You couldn't wait to get away from here."

Speaking of slaps to the back of his head. "What I felt..." Tyler looked up at the Colonel. "It wasn't the house I had problems with."

The other man's silence went on a beat too long. "I know."

God knows they'd locked horns every five minutes during Tyler's teenage years. But the actual *why* behind the horn-locking never actually came up. Until, it would appear, now.

Boomer wandered into the room, flopping down with a groan at Tyler's feet. "It wasn't you I was mad at. It was the situation."

"Knew that, too."

Air rushed from Tyler's lungs as he collapsed against the chair's squishy, welcoming back. "I was a total dirtbag, wasn't I?"

A half smile creasing weathered cheeks, the Colonel sat on one of the boxes, patting his knee for the dog to come get a scratch. "You were scared, Ty. And, yeah, angry. Can't blame you for that. And who else were you going to take it out on besides me and Jeannie? Me, especially. Since I wasn't about to let you play the victim card."

"But you just said—

"There can only be one good cop," he said, his lips

curving again. "And that was Jeannie. That doesn't mean I didn't sympathize with you. You got dealt a crap deal, Ty. No doubt about it. And I know…" He paused, scrubbing the heel of his hand over his jaw before linking his hands between his spread knees. "I should've said this a long time ago…but I'm proud of you. Of all you guys, but especially you."

Ty flinched. "Holy hell. Are you dying or something?"

The old man chuckled. "Not today. That I know of, anyway. It's just… I don't know. Maybe it's the last chick leaving the nest. Turning seventy. Realizing how much my life's about to change. Again. Makes a person get all reflective. Crazy, huh?"

"Very."

"Not that I planned on saying all of this when I called you—I really do need you to help me load these boxes. But since you're here…"

The Colonel's knees creaked when he got up and went to the kitchen, returning with a couple of beers. Tyler pushed out a short laugh. "So we're drinking buddies now?"

"Whatever," Pop said, lowering himself to the box again, popping the tab to his can and taking a swallow as Tyler frowned at his own bottle.

"So…what on earth have I done to…" He looked up. "Earn your approval?"

"You sound skeptical."

"Not that there's a reason for that or anything," Tyler said, and the Colonel chuckled. Then he released a breath.

"Jeannie was always on my case about giving you guys space, trusting you'd make the right decisions. Except then this kid comes along with a chip on his shoulder the size of a damned redwood." He held up his hand. "And as we've already established, you had your reasons. Valid ones. But that didn't make trusting you easy. Because you could've made some really bad choices. And don't think Jeannie and I didn't hold our breaths that you wouldn't."

The old man took another sip of his beer, nudging the sacked-out dog's ribs with the tip of his loafer. Boomer sighed, and the Colonel smiled, looking back at Tyler. "But amazingly, you didn't. No, you didn't get the best grades. And God knows you did more than your share of stupid. But from your first job at sixteen, you worked your ass off, sucking every bit of knowledge you could out of whoever you worked for. And now you've got your own business at thirty. That's pretty damned impressive. For anybody."

Tyler felt his chest get tight. "I always thought you were pissed I didn't go to college."

"At first? Sure. Until I realized it would've never worked for you then. You weren't motivated. And damned if we were going to throw good money after bad."

Tyler had to laugh. "You're right. I would've flunked out before Thanksgiving."

"Thanksgiving, hell. You wouldn't've made it to homecoming. That doesn't mean you're not made of good stuff. Yeah, you're stubborn as hell, nobody can tell you what to do. But when *you* want to do something, nobody can stop you, either. Like all those jobs you got when you were still a kid. Figuring out how to write a business plan so the bank'd finance your buying the salvage company. Not to mention deciding to meet your birth mother. *That* took guts, son. Showed real maturity, too, moving past all that."

The beer soured in Tyler's gut as his adoptive father went on. "You've come a long way. A lot farther than I thought you might, frankly, when you stormed out of here when you were eighteen like you knew it all and I was the dumbest person on God's green earth. So, yeah, you turned out pretty damned good. And you know who'd be about to bust right now? Jeanne. Not that I'm any too sure there's a heaven, but if there is? She's looking down with a great big smile."

His face burning, Tyler hauled himself off the sofa, grabbing the tape dispenser from the coffee table. "So you want to load these tonight?"

Silence thrummed for several seconds until, grunting a little, the Colonel got to his feet. "Yeah, go ahead. I'll take 'em to the library first thing in the morning. They said they've got people to help unload."

The Colonel's words tumbling around inside Tyler's brain, they worked without talking for a while, Tyler piling the heavy boxes onto a handcart, then wheeling the loads out to the garage to heft them into the back of the Colonel's Jeep Cherokee. When they were done, the old man walked Tyler and Boomer back out front, looking more at peace than Tyler could remember since Jeanne's passing. Like something had released inside him.

"Thanks," he said. "Appreciate you coming over."

"Sure thing. Um…you need anything else, let me know, okay?"

"I'll do that."

To Tyler's shock, the Colonel then yanked him into a bone-crushing hug, releasing him a moment later to regard him so intently Tyler's face warmed all over again. And he heard himself say, "How the hell did you put up with me all those years?"

His reply was a deep chuckle. Then a shrug. "What was I supposed to do, send you back and ask for a better kid?"

"People do."

"The thought never even crossed my mind," he said softly. "Hanging you by your toes, once or twice, maybe. But not giving you up. Or giving up on you." He angled slightly away, his pale hair glowing in the moonlight filtering through the straggly, leftover clouds. "I know you never accepted me as your father. For many reasons, not the least of which was…well, maybe I didn't know how to be the father you needed." His gaze met Tyler's again. "But from the moment you walked into this house you were mine. And nothing can ever change that. Not even you."

Tyler felt like his chest was going to cave in. Because he knew that. Always had. Okay, perhaps not so much during those early days, when he'd felt like an expendable piece of crap. Hell, maybe that's why he'd challenged his foster dad's authority so hard, and so often, as a way of testing the relationship. Because how else could he be *really* sure he was wanted?

Not that he'd known at the time that's what he was doing, but now…

"I know, Pop," he breathed out. And for once the word didn't feel strange. Not as strange, anyway. "And I just want to say…" He took a deep breath. "Thanks for calling me your son."

"Even when you didn't want to hear it?"

"Especially then."

The corners of the Colonel's mouth curved, barely, before he squeezed Tyler's shoulder then walked back into the garage, the door slowly groaning shut behind him.

Tyler and Boomer slowly jogged back home through mostly quiet, now-dark streets, the silence only occasionally broken by the hissing of tires over still-wet blacktop. And as they ran, stuff jogged loose inside his brain, too, old hurts and resentments and fears, breaking off in big chunks and then…dissolving. Like clumps of sand in the ocean, their solidity only an illusion.

That in turn got him to thinking about his first summer with the Nobles, when they'd all gone to the shore and Jeanne had tried to teach him how to swim in the ocean. Except first he needed to learn how to float, which, it turned out, wasn't so easy. Because every time he'd start to sink he'd flail his skinny arms and legs, which of course only made him sink faster.

"Stop fighting, sweetie," Jeanne had said beside him, laughing, her patience as limitless as the sun-speckled sea itself. "Soon as you relax, the water will hold you up, I promise. Let go of what you *think* you know and trust the water to hold you. Trust *yourself....*"

And eventually he did learn to float, to trust what he didn't understand—

Breathing hard, Tyler stopped so suddenly Boomer spun around on his leash in front of them. Because that's exactly what he'd been doing, wasn't it? Flailing and thrashing to keep from sinking, even though the more he did the faster he sank, right back into that bottomless well of self-justification and defeat and hopelessness he'd barely kept his head above since he was a little kid.

Instead of trusting that letting himself float on this thing he didn't understand—that letting himself *love*—would *keep* him from drowning.

And somewhere in heaven, angels applauded.

Tyler almost laughed, even as something like fear gripped his heart so tightly he could barely breathe.

Holy hell—he loved Laurel.

He *loved* her.

Heart thumping, Tyler's gaze roamed the still, silent street as though he'd never seen it before. He loved her...as in, handing-over-his-heart-on-a-dented-platter love. Head-floating-off-his-body love. An I'm-gonna-freaking-die-without-this-woman love.

Not that—he frowned—he knew for certain that Laurel loved him. Again, not always easy to see something you're not looking for. Or maybe are afraid to see. And even if

she did, no way would she make the first move, given her
history. But if there was a chance…

Tyler punched out a misty breath into the damp night air.

If there was a chance, he had to take it. Had to risk it.
Because unless he did, unless he was willing to lay his
heart bare for her, even if she stomped on it—or, probably
more likely, laughed in his face—he didn't deserve her.

However.

He'd also heard, very clearly, her conditions for the *pos-
sibility* of there being more between them. Not that she'd
realized, probably, she'd been giving him an ultimatum.
Since she'd also, probably—given the pitying look in her
eyes—never thought the lightbulb would ever go off. But
even if she did laugh, or shake her head and walk away,
or slam the door in his face…she was still right about one
thing: it was time—way past time—for some heavy-duty
crap shoveling.

So he'd best grab his heaviest shovel and get on with it.

An hour later, showered and dressed in clean jeans and
a hoodie that didn't look like the dog'd been gnawing on
it, he rang Starla's doorbell. She answered a moment later,
her hand landing on her chest.

"Tyler! What—?"

"All these years," he said through a tight throat, "I've
been mad at you for giving me up. Instead of appreciat-
ing what you *gave* me. And I am so, so sorry for being
such a putz."

Even as her eyes watered, his mother covered her mouth
to stifle a giggle. Then she lowered it again, wrapping up
in her long sweater. "So…you want a sandwich or something?"

"Yeah, that'd be great," he said, stepping inside.

Chapter Twelve

"Good God," Gran said as she hauled Jonny out of his crib. "At this rate the kid's going to be playing for the Giants by the time he's six. And this is just from booby milk?"

"Yep," Laurel said, taking the baby from her grandmother before they both went down in a heap. "The plan is to breast-feed exclusively until he's six months."

"You gotta be kidding me? I had your mother on cereal at eight weeks." Laurel gave her a look, and she sighed. "Fine, you don't want an old lady's advice," she said, following Laurel down the hall to the living room, "I'm not gonna give it. They're your boobies...do whatever you want with them. But all this *do this, don't do that* malarkey—it changes every ten years. And somehow, the human race still keeps chugging along."

Lauren settled in the armchair and deftly unhooked her nursing bra, wincing slightly as Jonny eagerly latched on. Smiling down at her son, she sensed Gran lowering herself to the sofa a few feet away. As well as what was coming.

"So what's wrong?" her grandmother asked.

Yeah. That. Calmly, Laurel swiveled her gaze to Gran, today swathed from neck to ankle in turquoise velour. With pristine white running shoes to go with. "Why do you think—?"

"Like I haven't seen that expression a few times in the past thirty-six years."

"I get this weird feeling when my milk lets down. That's all. It passes."

"Yeah, well, unless your milk comes in every thirty seconds, I'm gonna say you're lying through your teeth. And how come you haven't mentioned Tyler once since I've been here?"

On a tight little laugh, Laurel looked out the window again. "Man, you're good."

"This, we know. So?"

She rearranged the baby's blanket. "He asked me to marry him."

There was actual silence. For about three seconds. "What? No, strike that. *And?*"

"And, nothing. I turned him down."

"Because…?"

"Because he's not in love with me?"

Another pause preceded, "But you're in love with him."

A tiny smile pushed at her lips. "I loved Mom dearly. But damned if I'm going to emulate her."

"This isn't the same situation. Not even remotely."

"True. Because Dad at least had a reason to marry Mom. Tyler doesn't even have that." She hesitated, then said, "We haven't even kissed. Let alone done anything else."

"Hmm. Okay, so maybe a bit old-fashioned. But not unworkable. And it's not as if you couldn't, what do they call that? Do a trial run?"

"Gran."

"What? You think I don't know about this stuff? That your grandfather and I didn't check out the goods before we plunked down the cash?"

"And I so didn't need to know that."

"Actually, considering your dilemma, I think you did."

Laurel sighed. "In any case...did Granddad ask you to marry him before you...plunked?"

"Wouldn't have plunked otherwise, cookie. That liberated, I wasn't. But I also knew he was crazy about me. Just like I was about him."

"Well, there you are. Not that I don't think there's some serious crazy going on here, but not that kind of crazy."

"Then why did he ask you? If you believe he doesn't love you—"

"Not believe, Gran. Know."

"You're sure about this?"

"Very."

Gran's lips scrunched together. "I don't get it. I've seen the guy around you. And the baby," she said, nodding toward the schlurping Jonny. "He's obviously very fond of you both—"

"Fond, yes. And he's a good guy who sincerely wants to *do* good. To maybe right some wrongs in his own life. But that's not a good enough foundation for a marriage—"

"And there you go again, Miss Picky," Gran said, pushing herself to her feet. "Honestly, child! The man asks you to marry him—a good man, like you said, someone who's clearly nuts about Jonny—and you turn him down? Have you lost your freaking marbles?"

"Already established that. Except believe it or not, this isn't about me."

"Really."

"Fine, so not totally about me. But I do have a child to consider, who doesn't need to go through what I did, watching a marriage die a slow, and very painful, death. And that's what would happen, when Tyler eventually realized he'd made a mistake."

"So you can read the future now?"

"No. But I'd like to think I've learned from the past. And you know what? Tyler doesn't need to go through this, either. Especially since this isn't what he wants, not really—it's what he thinks he should do. For reasons I couldn't even begin to explain, since I don't live in his head. And if rejecting an offer I know is only going to cause pain down the road makes me *picky*...then I'll have to live with that."

"For the rest of your life. Alone."

"Maybe so, Gran. And I'm as fully prepared to live with the consequences of that choice as I am with the consequences of this one," she said, slightly hoisting the baby. "But what you don't understand is..."

Her eyes tearing, she glanced down at Jonny. "Despite what you might think, this isn't about whether I think Tyler's good enough for me. Because, trust me, he passed *good enough* ages ago. Not perfect, no. But then, who the hell wants perfect? Like I need the pressure to live up to that, right?"

"Oh, sweetie..." Gran came and sat on the little ottoman in front of Laurel, laying a hand on her knee. "Then what's the problem?"

"The problem is that *Tyler* doesn't think he's good enough. Which means I could love him, and trust him, and believe in him until the cows come home, but if he docsn't believe in himself..." She shook her head. "Kinda hard to fix someone who thinks he's permanently broken. Even if I could—"

The doorbell rang. Gran frowned. "You expecting company?"

"No. Probably somebody selling magazines. Or salvation. You can see out the corner of the window, though…"

Groaning a little, Gran got up again and hobbled to the window, where her hand went to her throat. "Holy Toledo, you are not gonna believe this."

"What is it?"

"Not what. Who." Gran turned to her. "And I'm guessing he ain't selling magazines."

Tyler changed out the lightbulbs in Starla's bedroom overhead as she made the sandwiches—roast beef on rye with her own horseradish sauce—then sat at her kitchen table when she called. Some old pine thing she'd scavenged from the curb after her neighbors moved out last winter, he remembered, then refinished. Same as she'd done with the brightly painted, mismatched chairs. In fact, nearly everything in the house had been rescued and repurposed…a trait he'd apparently inherited.

And as they ate, they talked. Really talked for a change, instead of dancing around topics neither had wanted to deal with.

Or rather, he really listened.

And as he listened, he decided he might actually learn to like this woman he'd once loved, who'd caused him so much pain and confusion, whom he'd blamed for so long for his doubts and fears. The dull, dreamy gaze he remembered from his childhood was long gone, revealing an intelligence underneath the ditziness he'd refused to see. Much like what he'd seen in Laurel's eyes from day one. The intelligence, that is, not the ditziness. The very thing that had most attracted him.

That now made him want to finally get his head screwed on straight.

"I'd met the Nobles, you know," Starla said when they

were halfway through their makeshift dinner, pouring him a glass of milk, then plunking a bag of SunChips between them before sitting back down. "And it was so obvious that they could give you a thousand times more than I ever could, sober or not. You have to believe that what I did, I did for you. Even…even when I barely had two non-doped-up brain cells to rub together, I loved you. What I wasn't—or at least, didn't feel at the time—was worthy of you. So I gave you to people who were. Simple as that. My mistake—and there were many—was thinking you'd understand."

With that, the last of the anger and resentment finally sloughed off as Tyler finally got himself out of the way enough to see the situation through his mother's eyes… the eyes of someone who'd only been trying to make the best of things. For *him,* not herself.

"I was ten," he said gently.

"I know, but…" She smiled. "You were such a smart kid, Ty. So smart it scared me sometimes, the way you'd catch on about stuff that went right over my head. I loved you, but I didn't know how to give you what you needed. Which I realized even more after I got clean than before."

Not sure what to say about that, Tyler leaned back in his chair. That huge cat of hers writhed around his calf under the table, making some bizarre sound more like a rusty spring than a meow. Distractedly he lowered his hand to meet the beast's head bump, then said, "Why *wouldn't* you tell me about my father? And I'm not asking that to find out about him—frankly, I no longer care—"

"Really?"

"Crazy, right? But it's true. All that…it really doesn't matter anymore. I had—have—a father. Even if I didn't want to accept that," he said with a smirk. "What I still want to know, though, is what was going on in *your* head."

"It's really that important?"

"Yeah. It is."

After poking at her own sandwich for a moment, Starla said, "When you showed up at Costco, said who you were…" Her eyes lifted to his. "I thought I'd gotten a miracle. You wanting to connect again…it was far more than I expected. Than I *deserved*. Except I quickly figured out you had an ulterior motive, that what you really wanted was to find out about your father. And I was the only way that was going to happen."

The guilt screaming in her eyes only poked at his own. "And that didn't bother you?"

"Hell, yes, it cut me to shreds. But beggars can't be choosers, right?"

At that point, he was feeling a little shredded himself. "So…you deliberately didn't answer my questions so I'd keep asking."

"Bingo. Because after all that time, I couldn't bear losing you again. Not that I ever really had you. Obviously. And I'm not proud of that, that I deliberately kept the truth from you. Then again, I wasn't proud of what the answer would have been, either, so my evasion was…multilayered, shall we say." Frowning, Tyler stared at the remains of his sandwich for several moments until she said, "No comment?"

He felt his mouth pull to one side. "We were playing each other, weren't we?"

"Guess so." Then she said softly, "And you've got your frowny face on again."

An old memory stirred, of her saying that to him when he was little, making him smile. "Because…I don't know. On some level I understand what you're saying. But there's still part of me that wonders if…if I'd been different, things would've turned *out* different." At her puckered brow, he said, "If I hadn't been too much for you to handle."

"Of course you were too much for me to handle! Because I couldn't handle myself...." Then she gasped. "Oh, honey—you don't think I started using *because* of you? Or that I gave you up..." Horror bloomed in her eyes. "Ohmygod, no! *No.* Now you listen to me..."

His mother grabbed his hand again, holding on tight. "I was a mess because of my own choices, choices that controlled me instead of the other way around. You were the *best* little guy, as a baby. So...so *patient* with me, always smiling and laughing. But I was alone, and overwhelmed...." Tears glittered in her eyes. "If anything, you starting acting out because of *me.* Frankly I'm surprised—and grateful, believe me—that you didn't get in worse trouble than you did. And when they found you wandering by yourself that night and took you away... You bet, I was relieved. But not for my sake. For yours. And then, after I got out of rehab..."

Her lips pressed together. "I was scared, Ty. Scared I'd slip back into old habits. God knows I wanted to stay clean, but I wasn't sure I could. And if I'd regained custody and screwed up again, I would have never forgiven myself. You weren't a bad kid, Tyler. I was a bad mother."

His throat aching, Tyler cupped his hand over hers, clearly startling her. "A *bad* mother wouldn't have made that kind of sacrifice. And I'm sorry it's taken me twenty years to figure that out."

Her throat working overtime, she finally nodded, then got up to clear their plates, hauling a carton of vanilla ice cream out of her bottom freezer. "Still like hot fudge sundaes?" she asked.

"You bet."

She pulled a jar of sauce and a can of whipped cream from the fridge, clunking the sauce into the microwave. As it whirred, she said, not looking at him, "I was eighteen.

Your father was in his thirties. And married. His wife was pregnant. And yes, it was stupid… I was stupid for getting involved to begin with, for believing the promises…" Her mouth flattened. "He offered to pay for the abortion." The microwave beeped. She turned to him, tears in her eyes. "I got all the way to the clinic, had even gone through the preliminary exam before…before I changed my mind."

Slowly, Tyler got up from the table, going to his mother and pulling her into his arms, rocking her against his chest for a while before saying, "Whatever happened to him, do you know?"

Her hair tickled his chin as she shook her head.

"Then screw 'im," he said, and she softly laughed before pulling away to finish up their sundaes.

"So what brought this all on, anyway?" she asked, handing him his dish of ice cream. When he didn't respond, she said, "Unless it's none of my business—"

"No, it's not that. It's…" He returned to the table, poking his spoon into the gooey ice cream and sauce for a moment before looking at his mother. "It's a whole bunch of stuff, I guess, all ganging up on me."

Starla smiled slightly. "And is Laurel part of that?"

Tyler blew out a breath. "Yeah."

After spooning in a bite of her sundae, his mother said quietly, "She knows, doesn't she? About me?"

"Yeah. *Now.*"

"So I guess you figured out she was baiting you? When you two gave me a ride the other day?"

One side of his mouth pulled up. "Not until after she confronted me later, no. I mean, yeah, that conversation was doing a real number on my head. But I'm pretty good at not hearing what I don't want to hear."

"Then maybe it's time you got over that."

"Working on it," he said, and his mother tipped her spoon at him. Then she stabbed at her ice cream again.

"Is Jonny yours?"

"No," Tyler said on a dry laugh. "Laurel was pregnant when we met. Daddy's not in the picture. And anyway, we haven't..." He blushed. "We're friends."

"But you'd like to be more."

It took a moment to find his voice. "Not that I have any idea if she feels the same way."

"Only one way to find out, right?"

"Right," Tyler said, then stood, leaning over to kiss his mother's forehead. She looked up, startled—it was the first time he'd kissed her since he was little.

And for the first time since then, he felt whole.

Or at least, enough to risk making a damn fool of himself.

Pulling onto his street, Tyler frowned at the silver Lexus parked in front of Laurel's house. Frowned harder when he passed and saw the out-of-state plates, felt his hair rise on the back of his neck. And right then, the only thing stronger than the fear that suddenly swamped him, was the anger.

And let's work with that, shall we?

He parked the truck, his breathing ragged as he stood in the driveway, only half hearing Boomer's mad whining and scratching from inside. Tyler almost felt like he was being physically held back from storming over to Laurel's. But it definitely would not serve his purpose to go in with guns blazing like some idiot—

Laurel's door opened. And sure enough, a man emerged. Tallish. Thin. Definitely older, although it was hard to tell in the porch light. Tyler's gut clenched when the man touched her arm, leaned down to kiss her cheek.

He couldn't hear what they were saying. Didn't care.

He waited until Laurel's door closed to walk across the yard, hand extended. "You must be Barry," he said, and the man flinched.

"Uh...yeah." He ignored Tyler's outstretched hand. "And you must be the neighbor. Tyler, is it?"

Tyler withdrew his hand, slamming it into his jeans' pocket. Better than where he wanted to slam it. "Yep. So I take it you came to your senses?"

"Wow. You don't pull any punches, do you?" Barry said, and Tyler thought, *You should only know.* "But I guess you could say I did. In fact—" he smiled "—I just asked Laurel to marry me."

A red haze turned the streetlamp the color of blood and Barry's face into a devil's mask. To think at one time Tyler'd actually volunteered to find this creep, make him own up to his responsibility. Now all he saw was a thief.

"Man, you are one piece of work," he said quietly, and Barry's eyebrows shot up.

"Excuse me—?"

"You let her go through the whole pregnancy alone, didn't even tell her where you freaking *were,* and now you waltz back into her life like some damn Prince Charming and ask her to *marry* you? Congratulations on winning the douchebucket of the year award—"

"Now, hold on—"

Tyler came closer in the damp grass, making the guy back up. "Where were you when she needed someone to paint the nursery? When she went into labor in the middle of the night and needed a ride to the hospital? Were you there when your son was born? Were you? Because I sure as hell don't remember seeing you. And all those nights when the kid had colic so bad he'd cry for hours on end— were you there to walk him, to give Laurel some relief? Yeah. That's right. You weren't. And where the *hell* were you when Jonny..." To his extreme annoyance, his throat clogged. "When he smiled for the first time?"

"You don't understand—"

"Oh, believe me, I understand. I understand a helluva lot better than you have any idea." His arms crossed over his chest. "So now what? You've had an epiphany or something? Or an attack of guilty conscience? So you think that by marrying Laurel you'll make it all good?" He held up one hand. "And if she does, God knows that's her decision. She loved you when you two made Jonny, so for all I know she still does. But as far as I'm concerned you're—"

"Tyler! Stop!"

He whipped around to see Laurel standing on the porch, wrapped in a sweater with her arms strangling her stomach. "I turned him down, you idiot."

"What?"

Her mouth twitched. "I said no."

His eyes cut back to Barry: "So why the hell didn't you say that?"

"You didn't exactly give me a chance, did you?" Then the other man extended his hand, giving Tyler's a firm shake as he quietly, and almost sadly, said, "Take good care of them," before walking back to his car.

Tyler was up the stairs before the man could drive off, his hands cupping Laurel's face, his heart feeling like it was going to punch through his chest. "Why did you turn him down?"

Her eyes glistened. "Turns out, my heart doesn't know from practical," she said, and his mouth dropped to hers, not gently, not gently at all, and she kissed him back every bit as not-gently...until she clamped his upper arms and pulled away, her eyes searching his.

Then she smiled. "Really?"

And in that smile, Tyler saw *exactly* what he was looking for.

"Oh, hell, yeah," he said, his heart bouncing around in his chest like Boomer when he got excited, and she laughed and linked her arms around his neck and kissed him even more fiercely than he'd kissed her, probably more fiercely, actually, than any woman had ever kissed a guy in the history of making out, holy crap, and he was enjoying the hell out of it, too…until somebody drove by and honked at them.

"Jersey, gotta love it," he said, and she laughed and grabbed his hand and tugged him inside, where he butt-shut the door and yanked her against him again, the happiest he'd been in his entire life. Then he took her hand and placed it in the center of his chest, pinning it there with his own, and she gave him a quizzical smile.

"You feel that?" he whispered. "That's what a whole heart feels like."

The smile softened. "All fixed?"

"Definitely getting there."

"What can I do to help things along?" she asked, unzipping his hoodie, and he laughed. Then stilled.

"The baby—"

"Sound asleep," she murmured. "It's all good."

Or sure as hell promised to be, he thought, realizing she'd begun to tug his T-shirt free from his pants, and while his heart—among other things—leaped with joy, he had just enough functioning brain cells left to grab her hands again. When she looked up, confused, he touched his forehead to hers, sucked in a breath big enough to inflate a Macy's parade float, and said, "Before you have your wicked way with me, there's something I need to say."

Smiling, she freed one hand to fork it, trembling, through his hair. "You're not really a blond?"

Even as he laughed, his eyes burned. Along with the rest of him. "No. I mean, yes. I mean…" He heaved a breath. "I love you."

"Yeah, got that—"

"No, I needed to say it out loud. Because…I never have. To anyone. Not as an adult, anyway."

Tears crested on her lower lids. "Aw…I'm your f-first?"

"And last," he said softly, barely touching her temple, like she'd disappear if he pressed too hard. "I love you so much…it's like my body, my brain…they're not big enough to hold it all."

"Then share it," she whispered, palming his face and kissing him lightly on the lips. "With me. Right now. Because I love you, too, you big goofball. And I'm about to burst with holding it in."

"So…what're you saying?"

She snorted. "I'm about to let you see my stretch marks. What do you think I'm saying? And why the *hell* are we talking?"

"Got it," he said, leading her to her bedroom, only to groan. "What am I thinking? I didn't expect… I mean, I don't have—"

He turned to her, and words fled. Because Laurel had wriggled out of her jeans. "Bathroom." Then she whisked off her top. "Medicine chest."

Tyler realized he was staring. "I'm not talking about mouthwash, honey."

"Neither am I, studmuffin." Then, frowning, she followed his gaze to the cleavage spilling over a bra that looked like something a nun might've worn. She lifted her eyes. "What?"

"Breast-feeding does that?"

"Amazing, right? Anyway…" Taking him by the hand, she led him down the hall and to the bathroom, where she carefully opened the squeaky medicine cabinet door and made like some game show chick. "Ta-da! Gran gave them to me after the baby came."

In awe, Tyler reached for the box of condoms. "You have no idea how much I love that woman right now."

"Actually, I do."

Then he grabbed *her* hand and hustled them both back to the bedroom, where by this time they were stifling their laughter like a couple of pranking teenagers, and then they were naked and he couldn't believe how freaking beautiful she was, the way motherhood glowed through her now even more than when she'd been pregnant…and he ached with wanting to be inside her, with wanting *her*…this…*them*.

And yet, oddly, he was in no hurry, either, enjoying the hell out of every kiss and touch and stroke, both given and received, smiling at her sighs, grinning full out when she somehow flipped him on his back and straddled him, and her touch was magic, driving him crazy and soothing him at the same time. Yowsers.

"Been thinking about this for a while, have you?" he whispered, and she grinned.

"You might say… Oh!"

He'd sat up, his back against her headboard, tugging her into his lap so things sorta automatically fit together without anybody having to think about it too hard, but also so she could control the whole how much/how fast thing, and it was good, so very, very good.…

And in the dim light from the living room her eyes met his as she took him all the way inside, and it wasn't like sex at all, it was like…like she was wrapping him up in her soul. Damn. Then everything stilled, suspended, and it was just them, just this moment, her scent and her breath and the soft, warm feel of her around him…and she smiled and lowered her mouth to his, then lifted it enough to whisper, "Thank you," against his lips....

Then she nodded and closed her eyes, and Tyler held her so close absolutely nothing could even think of getting between them, and his last coherent thought before the world went *kablam,* was *Oh,* hell, *yes.*

Wanting to hold on to the moment like a kid might a firefly in a glass jar, Laurel lay absolutely still in Ty's arms, feeling his heartbeat pound under her hand, against her ear.

"You okay?" he whispered, gently fingering her tangled hair away from her temple, and she lifted her head to look into his eyes, and joy flickered inside her like a *thousand* fireflies.

"What I am right now..." She smiled, remembering. "I think Gran would call it *ooh-là-là.*"

Chuckling, Tyler wrapped his arms more tightly around her to lay his cheek in her hair, and she felt so at peace, so loved and cherished and freaking *happy*....

"Yeah, that's pretty much covers it," he whispered. "Because it was more than the sex being good. I mean, it was, absolutely, don't get me wrong, but...hell. Words seem so...dumb."

Feeling ridiculously pleased with herself, with *life,* Laurel toyed with a curl of his chest hair for a moment, then said, "Here's a thought—maybe it has something do with, I don't know..." she raised her head again "—being in love?"

He grinned, teasing. "You think maybe?"

"Could be. Although we should probably test our theory a few more times. Just to be sure."

"Because that would be the logical thing to do."

"That would be my take on it. But...to be honest..." Reluctantly, she pulled herself to a sitting position. "Not tonight. I have the feeling I'm going to be sore later."

"Oh, hell, I'm sorry—"

"Sore, not incapacitated. And it's not like tonight was our only shot."

Silence. Then she heard him sit up, too. "You're saying this without even knowing why I'm here."

She twisted to face him. "I know why you're here, you already said. Knew before that, when I heard you talking to Barry. That's what's important. The details—" she shrugged "—not so much."

"But you need to know…I'm not the same man who proposed to you before."

"Oh, sweetie…" Laurel touched his face. "You're *exactly* the same man who asked me to marry him before. The man I fell in love with weeks ago, the man I knew was underneath all the junk up here—" she skimmed a knuckle along his temple then palmed his heart "—and here." Tyler covered her hand with his; she could see his throat working overtime. She ducked her head to look in his eyes. "And you're really sure the junk's gone?"

"Completely? I don't know." A smile touched his lips as he pulled her against him again. "But at least it's not blocking my view anymore."

Then she listened, while he told her about his conversation with the Colonel. His mother. And she could hear in his voice the pain and resentment and anger releasing him. Or his releasing them, whichever, the result was the same: he was finally free. Free to love and be loved. To be not only the man she needed, but the man he needed to be.

"And if it weren't for you," he said softly, nuzzling the top of her head as they lay there, "who knows if I would've ever figured out what an idiot I was being."

"I live to serve," she said, and he quietly chuckled.

"So Barry actually asked you to marry him?"

"He actually did. Go figure. Thirty-six years old, not a

marriage proposal in sight, and then, boom, two in a row. Go, me."

"And were you at least tempted to accept?"

"*Pfft,* not even for a nanosecond. Besides, it was only about Barry having a lightbulb moment. Except his moment was far more about guilt than any revelation that he loved me. Unlike other people in this room." She snuggled closer. "Like I said, I'm not up for being anybody's means of atonement. Go work out your issues, *then* we'll talk. And if you're too late…not my problem."

"So you tossed him out on his ass."

"You don't have to sound quite so happy about that."

"You kidding? He lost. I won. Happy, hell. I'm *ecstatic.*"

Laurel chuckled. "He's still Jonny's birth father, so if he wants to be part of his son's life, I won't stand in his way. But as you said, he wasn't there for the birth. Or the colic. Or any of it. By his choice. And you were. By *your* choice. And that's what makes a daddy. Not DNA."

After a very long pause, Tyler said, "I know," and Laurel knew he was talking about the man who'd been there for him through *his* hell. As Tyler would be there for whatever shenanigans Jonny put them through.

Them. Not just *her.*

"Hey," she said, her eyes watering, "shouldn't you go get Boomer? Because you can't very well leave him alone in the house all night, right?"

Tyler stilled. "You want me to spend the night?"

She shifted in his arms, her hand on his chest. "I want you to spend every night. But I wouldn't want to presume."

He did a fist pump, which made her laugh, before he leaned in for another kiss. And, judging from where his hand was headed, a lot more. Giggling against his mouth, she pushed his shoulder and sat up. "Go get your dog, I'm not going anywhere."

"Be right back," he said, lightly kissing her lips before getting up to yank on the essential items of clothing— jeans, shoes, hoodie—and disappearing, a moment before she heard somebody's little "Feed me!" chirp from across the hall.

And she smiled.

Tyler and Boomer returned a few minutes later, the lamebrained dog practically knocking Tyler over in his rush to get to Laurel and the baby as they nestled into one corner of her sofa. And the air left Tyler's lungs, the way the pair of them glowed in the soft light from the end-table lamp, like one of those old Italian Madonna and child paintings.

"Boomer! No!" he shout-whispered as the dog schlurped his tongue across Jonny's downy little head, then jumped up on the sofa to flop down as close to Laurel as he could get, belly up, stump wiggling. "Forget it, dog," Tyler said as he lugged the beast off the sofa and onto the floor...only to instantly take his place, slinging an arm around Laurel's shoulders and gently pulling her close as he watched the baby, tiny fingers tightly curled around one of hers as he suckled away. And he thought, as his heart fisted, *I would kill for these people.*

His *family.* And not some pieced-together thing, either, no sir. Because this was as real and solid and whole as it got.

His eyes burning, he brushed his lips across her temple, laying his cheek in her hair.

"What are you thinking?" she asked.

"About asking you to marry me again."

"For reals, this time?"

"Absolutely, for reals. As in, a real church wedding, with you in a real wedding dress, and me in a real monkey suit, and Kelly can cook her heart out, and we'll dance our first dance to Ella Fitzgerald's 'At Last.' Since most of the guests will be over eighty."

"It sounds perfect," she said with a soft laugh.

"So is that a yes?"

"It's a *hallelujah,* is what it is," she said, and he laughed. Then, as the baby gurgled and the dog panted, she smiled into his eyes. "It almost feels wrong to be this happy."

And for the briefest moment, that old temptation whispered, *What makes you think you deserve this?*

And Tyler looked it smack in the eye and said right back, *Shut the hell up.*

"It's never wrong to be happy," he whispered, and, tears shining in her eyes, Laurel cupped his jaw and kissed him, and peace settled inside his soul like it was planning on sticking around for a good, long while.

* * * * *

COMING NEXT MONTH FROM

H HARLEQUIN®

SPECIAL EDITION

Available April 15, 2014

#2329 THE PRINCE'S CINDERELLA BRIDE
The Bravo Royales • by Christine Rimmer

Lani Vasquez cherishes her role as nanny to the Montedoran royal children—particularly since it offers proximity to her good friend, the handsome Prince Maximilian. Max has grieved his lost wife for years, but this Prince Charming is ready for the next chapter of his love story—and his Cinderella is right under his nose.

#2330 FALLING FOR FORTUNE
The Fortunes of Texas: Welcome to Horseback Hollow
by Nancy Robards Thompson

Christopher Fortune has gladly embraced the wealth and power of his newfound family name. But not everyone's as impressed by the Fortune legacy. His new coworker, Kinsley Aaron, worked for everything she ever got, and Chris's newly entitled attitude rubs her the wrong way. Now Chris will have to earn Kinsley's love—and his Fortune fairy-tale ending....

#2331 THE HUSBAND LIST
Rx for Love • by Cindy Kirk

Great job? Check. Hunky hubby? Not so much. Dr. Mitzi Sanchez has her life just where she wants it—except for the husband she's always dreamed of. She creates a checklist for her perfect man—but she insists pilot Keenan McGregor isn't it. With a bit of luck, Keenan might blow Mitzi's expectations sky-high....

#2332 HEALED WITH A KISS
Bride Mountain • by Gina Wilkins

Both burned by love, wedding planner Alexis Mosley and innkeeper Logan Carmichael aren't looking for anything serious when they plunge into a passionate affair. Little by little, though, what starts as a no-strings-attached fling evolves into something much deeper. Can they heal their emotional wounds to start afresh, or will the ghosts of relationships past haunt them forever?

#2333 GROOMED FOR LOVE
Sweet Springs, Texas • by Helen R. Myers

Due to her declining sight, Rylie Quinn abandoned her dreams of becoming a veterinarian and moved to Sweet Springs, Texas, as an animal groomer. She just wants to get on with her life—something that irritating attorney Noah Prescott won't allow her to do. He's determined to dig up Rylie's past, and, as he and Rylie butt heads, true love might just rear its own.

#2334 THE BACHELOR DOCTOR'S BRIDE
The Doctors MacDowell • by Caro Carson

Bright, free-spirited and bubbly, Diana Connor gets under detached cardiologist Quinn MacDowell's skin...and not in a way he'd care to admit. When the two are forced to work together at a field clinic, Quinn begins to see just how caring Diana is and how well she interacts with patients. This heart doctor might just need a bit of Diana's medicine for himself....

YOU CAN FIND MORE INFORMATION ON UPCOMING HARLEQUIN® TITLES, FREE EXCERPTS AND MORE AT WWW.HARLEQUIN.COM.

HSECNM0414

REQUEST YOUR FREE BOOKS!
2 FREE NOVELS PLUS 2 FREE GIFTS!

♦ HARLEQUIN®

SPECIAL EDITION
Life, Love & Family

HSE13R

*Lani Vasquez is a nanny to the royal children of
Montedoro...and nothing more, or so she thinks.
But widower Prince Maximilian Bravo-Calabretti
hasn't forgotten their single passionate encounter.
Can the handsome prince and the alluring au pair turn
one night into forever? Or will their love turn Lani into a
pumpkin at the stroke of midnight?*

***

He was fresh out of new tactics and had no clue how to get her to let down her guard. Plus he had a very strong feeling that he'd pushed her as far as she would go for now. This was looking to be an extended campaign. He didn't like that, but if it was the only way to finally reach her, so be it. "I'll be seeing you in the library—where you will no longer scuttle away every time I get near you."

A hint of the old humor flashed in her eyes. "I never scuttle."

"Scamper? Dart? Dash?"

"Stop it." Her mouth twitched. A good sign, he told himself.

"Promise me you won't run off the next time we meet."

The spark of humor winked out. "I just don't like this."

"You've already said that. I'm going to show you there's nothing to be afraid of. Do we have an understanding?"

"Oh, Max..."

"Say yes."

And finally, she gave in and said the words he needed to hear. "Yes. I'll, um, look forward to seeing you."

He didn't believe her. How could he believe her when she sounded so grim, when that mouth he wanted beneath his own was twisted with resignation? He didn't believe her, and he almost wished he could give her what she said she wanted, let her go, say goodbye. He almost wished he could *not* care.

But he'd had so many years of not caring. Years and years when he'd told himself that not caring was for the best.

And then the small, dark-haired woman in front of him changed everything.

***

Enjoy this sneak peek from Christine Rimmer's
THE PRINCE'S CINDERELLA BRIDE,
the latest installment in her Harlequin® Special Edition
miniseries **THE BRAVO ROYALES,** *on sale May 2014!*